God's Waiting Room

Larry Henry

McAnally Flats Press

McAnally Flats Press
Alcoa, Tennessee

God's Waiting Room
Copyright ©2025, Larry Henry
Copyright informational available upon request.
All rights reserved.
Cover Image © Shutterstock.com

Print: ISBN 979-8-9891249-2-3
Ebook: ISBN 979-8-9891249-3-0
Library of Congress Control Number: 2024926531

This novel is fiction. Except where permission has been granted, characters are the product of the author's imagination and are used fictitiously. Any resemblance between characters and real people, living or dead, is coincidental. Places and incidents are either fictitious or are cited fictitiously. The story cites some real events, facts, and places to support the plot, but the story is fiction and any resemblance to actual events is coincidental.

Except in the United States of America, this book is sold subject to the condition that it shall not, by way of trade or otherwise, be lent, resold, hired out, or otherwise circulated without the publisher's prior consent in any form of binding or cover other than that in which it is published and without a similar condition including this condition being imposed on the subsequent purchaser. The scanning, uploading, and distribution of this book via the Internet or via any other means without the permission of the publisher is illegal and punishable by law. Please purchase only authorized electronic editions, and do not participate in or encourage electronic piracy of copyrighted materials. Your support of the author's rights is appreciated.

First Edition, 2025, v.10

In memory of Bob Sams

Part 1
Soup Kitchen

CANADA

The dog lay silent on the front porch floor beside her master. She was a handsome animal with a large head, curly black fur, and intelligent blue eyes. Cooper weighs one hundred and twenty-seven pounds and is turning gray around the eyes and across her neck. The man purchased her from a tribesman five years ago down at the trading post. Since then he has trained the animal to be a guard dog. She is part wolf.

John Browning was watching five figures approaching from the far ridge. The men had come to kill him. They had not yet detected his position because the log cabin was camouflaged and was covered with snow. The Central Intelligence Agency wanted him dead because he knew too much. The cartel wanted him dead because he and Lakota had killed their top two personnel in their field office in Peachtree City, Georgia.

Browning had been a hired gun for Langley up until the top brass was offered $200,000 a month to look the other way. Browning found out and was fired then betrayed to the cartel.

The dog gave a low guttural sound, warning her master of the presence. He reached down from his rocking chair and scratches her head. The man loves the dog.

His daughter had been kidnapped by the cartel and sold into the sex trades. When he finally found her eight months later, she was addicted to the drugs they forced on her. Worst of all, she had become mentally unbalanced from the constant beatings and sexual abuse. She didn't recognize her father.

He took her away from the brothel after he killed the manager and one of his security guards. The second guard escaped through a rear window. Back in the mountains, he left his daughter with a Catholic convent in an ancient medieval castle near the town of Thunder Bay. When he returned to visit, he was informed she had taken her life. Shame had stolen his daughter, leaving behind a world of pain and regret. Afterward, he went deep into the Canadian mountains, leaving a trail of credit card signatures for the CIA to follow.

Inside the log cabin, he took down the special-made Swiss B&T rifle and filled the magazine with five .50 caliber cartridges. Back on the front porch, he made an adjustment to the telescopic sight. The specially polished lenses made it appear that he could reach out and touch the strangers on the far ridge. He waited for them to come closer.

He sighted in when they were well out in a snow-field. At 1,000 yards he squeezed the trigger. His target crashed backward into the snow. They ran but it was slow going in the deep drifts. He fired again. The man spun sideways and didn't move. The third man went down and began to crawl. He blew the man's head off. The fourth one fell to his knees, praying. He would allow that one to live to tell the others. He wanted them to be afraid. The fifth man died just as he reached the tree line.

John spoke to the dog. "We've got four days, Cooper, maybe a whole week. You'll like your new home. We'll be safe there. I have all your meds, mine too. They'll never find us back in that wilderness."

AFGHANISTAN

Fifty-nine hundred and thirty-seven miles east in Kandahar it was harvest time in the poppy fields. Hundreds of thousands of poppy plants grew on a seven-hundred-acre farm southeast of the city, not far from the Ahmad Shah Baba International Airport. Poppies are hearty plants and grow in abundance much like weeds.

Kandahar is the spiritual center for the Taliban. This is a male-dominated society in which women are allowed no education, nor the opportunity to work. The *burqa* must be worn at all times outside the home. High heels are forbidden for the clicking of heels might arouse a true believer. Thought Police patrol the streets. Strict adherence to Sharia Law is mandatory. Radical Islam has murdered over two million souls during the 20th Century.

So many opium pods grow on a single acre that it takes one man almost a week to harvest the opium gum from the pods. The paste is sometimes boiled then dried in the sun to produce opium powder. It can be refined into heroin, morphine, oxycodone, or any number of other opiates. Afghanistan produces over 80% of the world's opium and 95% of the heroin used in Europe.

Najibullah is the foreman for the opium farm. A bastard by birth, he had grown up hard in the streets of Afghanistan. He is a simple man, uneducated, and loyal to the Holy Quran. He stands six feet one, tall for a Muslim, and sports a full goatee to hide his shattered chin which was shot off thirteen years ago fighting the Americans in the Afghan War.

The soldiers call him 'No Chin.' None dare say that to his face for he is a powerful man and quick to anger. He was made foreman because of his size and dogged loyalty to his Taliban chieftain. The soldiers hate him because he is crude and blames them for his mistakes.

The military base is two kilometers from the poppy farm. Each year they harvest between 200,000 and 220,000 pounds of the poppy gum. One kilogram sells for $200 which is a lot of money in Afghanistan. The cost of operating the military base accounts for twenty-six percent of the sale of the poppy residue.

"Amir, we made extra on our sale to the Spaniard. He paid $2,120 for ten kilos. There is a Frenchman coming tomorrow who asks for ninety kilos. I will ask a little more and see if he agrees."

"It is a wise man who sells the seeds of destruction to his enemy. You have done well, Abdul."

"Yes, Amir. Tomorrow we spread more hardship among the infidels. It is Allah's will that we do these things. Allah will reward us with many virgins in Paradise."

"The thought of Paradise intrigues me. We will be very happy when we go there, and there will be women, Abdul, beautiful Arab women."

"And only true believers, great one. No kosher Jews and no blaspheming Christians."

"Our Iranian brothers need our help. I will send them some of the profits."

"Tehran is no more. The oil fields are silent. How can we deliver vengeance against the infidels?"

"Have faith, Abdul. Allah will find a way. Prostrate yourself while I pray."

"Oh blessed Allah. Grant us vision and wisdom. Show us the entrance and protect our passage that we may sow fire and brimstone upon the unbelievers. And grant us safe escape so we can return and spread your holy word. Peace be upon our people, and mercy and the blessings of Allah."

"That was a fine prayer, Yusuf. Surely Allah will grant us a sign."

HISTORY 2031, AD

The span of 2024 – 2027 had taken a grisly toll. Civil War dead numbered 39,000,000, mostly from starvation. The American Marxists had been soundly defeated. The Civil War in China had been just as devastating as what the US suffered. Upwards of 41,000,000 Chinese had perished. It was a time of much sadness but there was also hope. The citizens of both countries were no longer under Marxist control.

America had regained her energy independence. And China was getting all the oil and gas she needed from Russia and Indonesia. The rest of the world was at peace, with the exception of Radical Islam. Mexico once again had become the drug conduit into the United States.

Donald Trump had retired to his estate in Florida following the Civil War. Ron DeSantis was America's president. Victor Davis Hanson was chosen as vice president. Field Marshal Feng passed away in 2029. General Hu, Marshal Feng's brother, helped Johnny Poe become the new chairman of a free China. There was trust and friendship between the two mightiest nations on earth.

Young people adopted the old ways of dress. Bell-bottom jeans became all the rage. Poodle skirts and blouses, tank tops, loafers, one-button sport jackets with cuff-less slacks, cinched-waist dresses, and fedora hats. Drive-in restaurants reappeared, thousands of them. And patriotism. God returned to the classroom and the Pledge of Allegiance. People knew their neighbors and went to church on Sundays. Folks were thankful just to be alive following the horrors of the fighting.

THE FAR COUNTRY

John Browning used a Land Rover to travel back into the mountains. He had taken that route many times to stock his safe house. It took him and Cooper nine hours to get there. When they reached the mountain pass, they gazed down on a majestic panorama of snow, ice, and evergreen trees.

The log cabin was old from ages past with a stone fireplace. Repairs had been made and food and kerosene brought in. Perishables were stored next door in an abandoned silver mine that kept them fresh. Explosives were kept there too. The man was set for the duration until he heard from Lakota. His only connection to the outside world was a shortwave radio. The man on the other end of the radio was Lakota Kidwell, his former rifle range instructor at Parris Island.

"You sure we're safe?"

"We're good. I got a military jammer hooked up."

"Word I get, they're hot to trot over at the Agency. Probably scared shitless you're gonna rat 'em out. They'll send others."

"That's the plan. We have unfinished business with Langley and Mexico."

"We'll need backup. I'll round up some men."

"Be careful who you choose. We have to keep this under our hat."

"I know a dozen hardtails that fit the bill."

"That should do the job."

"I'll map out an itinerary."

"The north wall is close to the river."

"I'll be in touch. Love to Cooper."

John Browning went outside and sat huddled with his companion on a patch of green moss, watching the sun disappear behind a snowcapped mountain range. The scene resembled a portrait, serene and pure from any interference by man.

He thought back to his daughter and how she must have suffered. That always brought tears to his eyes. Cooper laid her head in his lap to comfort her master. He smiled then, remembering the young woman as a little girl. His wife Gabrielle was his sanctuary, his spiritual foundation. She completed him as a man. Their child had been the icing on their wedding cake.

The military base had a playground for kids and a swimming pool. They often took picnics there. Then the war came. Following the conflict, the CIA hired John.

SOUP KITCHEN

Nine individuals comprised the undercover team.

Vice President Victor Davis Hanson Senator Ted Cruz Brigadier General Penelope Steele, Commandant, Parris Island Master Sergeant Lakota Kidwell, Parris Island Major Mika Kidwell, Parris Island Captain John Browning, Parris Island First Lieutenant Gabrielle Browning, Parris Island Master Sergeant James Buckner, Chief Chef, Parris Island Staff Sergeant Roy Jones, Sous-Chef, Parris Island

Crystal City, Texas: A soup kitchen was established to attract cartel members from across the Rio Grande River. The poverty level was 36% following the war, so it appeared authentic, thirty-five miles from the Texas border. A bankrupt cafeteria was located southwest of downtown. Marine Corps spit and polish had the place ready for business in four days.

"Look at that crowd outside. We got customers comin' early."

"Go let 'em in. It's cold out there."

"Come on in, folks. Breakfast will be ready in a jiffy."

"Did you cook those eggs with bacon grease?"

"Sure did, with chopped green onions too. And link sausage and those potatoes and onions you like."

"You gonna spoil these folks, Gunny. We may have to adopt 'em."

"I bet some of them would make good Marines."

"Okay, folks, get in line an' grab a tray."

Breakfast and lunch patrons numbered seventy-three their first day.

Day Three. The lunch line had just formed with about twenty people standing in line. A tough-looking Mexican came in, went to the head of the line, jerked the tray away from a farmer wearing bib overalls, and shoved him aside.

Gunny came around the end of the service counter, snatched the tray, slamming it down on the countertop, grabbed the man by his shirt collar, and escorted him back outside. The Mexican pulled a switchblade, slicing Gunny's left forearm. Gunny knocked him out cold and left him lying on the sidewalk. When Gunny came back inside and closed the door, he was greeted with a standing ovation. After Gunny's arm was bandaged, everyone finished their meal. Customers for the day numbered one hundred and two.

A week went by without further incidents. Feeding poor folks became a joy for everyone involved.

Day 10. Lunch was half over when a Mercedes pulled up in front in the No Parking Zone. A well-dressed man and two sinister-looking characters stepped out. Gunny met them at the door. Roy Jones came up and sat down at a front table. He held a .45 automatic beneath his kitchen apron.

"You the owner of this shithole?"

"I am the proud owner of this shithole."

Gunny's response flustered the man. He expected a confrontation.

"You disrespected one of my men last week."

"That punk-ass with a knife had it coming."

"You broke his jaw."

"Good!"

"He said you threw him out because he's Mexican."

"He's lying. Look around. What do you see in here?"

The patrons comprised about thirty percent Mexican families. The man addressing Gunny realized he had made mistake. He bowed his head in disgust.

"I apologize, Mister. I should have known Marco got into a fight."

"Apology accepted. Would you like to come in and eat?"

"Yes, we would. That is very generous of you."

Later that afternoon, after the food was put away and the dishes all washed, Roy Jones gathered the men together in the dining area. Gunny was sitting on a tabletop with his feet resting on the bench.

"Our soup kitchen has turned into a big success. I'm very proud of you people. Today we served one hundred and fifty-one customers. Some of those folks haven't eaten a square meal in a coon's age.

"But that's not why we're here.

"There's a drug cartel about forty-six miles from here across the river. That man today in the Mercedes is the leader. He goes by the name El Diablo. His cartel and everyone in it is our objective. This operation is very hush-hush all the way up the line into Washington. You're not to breathe a word of this to anyone. If found out, we could all get killed. Anybody got a question?"

"Gunny, how are we supposed to get inside that place?"

"We're banking on them bribing us to use our trucks after we unload our supplies. An eighteen wheeler can haul a lot of drugs. Once they get used to our trucks coming and going, we'll ride through the front gate inside one of our rigs. That way we won't have to shoot our way in."

"They ain't but fourteen of us. Is that enough to get the job done, sir?"

"The Texas Rangers will block the highway and follow us in. They'll be another squad of Marines coming in from the river."

"How many guards, ya reckon?"

"We estimate fourteen or fifteen. The lab has two chemists."

"Why so few of us, Gunny?"

"This is a secret operation. We're going to burn everything, the house, the lab, the warehouse, and a barracks building. The main house is supposed to have a dozen people inside, five of them women. We're to spare the five women and waste the men."

The men fell silent. They had never been given such an order. Finally, Mississippi spoke up.

"Did this come out of Washington?"

"No, nine of us made that decision at Parris Island. It sends a message to stay the hell out of our United States."

The men huddled among themselves for a minute. Then Two Guns addressed his Master Sergeant.

"It's a good plan, sir. We like it. My little sister and her best friend died from fentanyl poisoning."

PARRIS ISLAND

General Steele: "I'm pleased to hear your men are happy serving the underprivileged. The poor suffered terribly under Obama and Joe Biden. What about that drug lord?"

Master Sergeant Buckner: "One of his thugs came in and caused a scene. I took him outside and kicked his ass. A few days later El Diablo shows up accusing me of throwing the bum out because he's Mexican. I straightened him out then invited him and his two bodyguards in to eat. That broke the ice. I believe he'll be back for the trucks."

"Good job, Gunny. I worry about you and the men dealing with those dirtbags. I'll go ahead and send the weapons. What do you need?"

"Let me see ... two boxes of grenades, one M2 Browning, thirteen M27 rifles, one M14 sniper rifle, two .45s, fourteen helmets, and fourteen vests.

Send extra ammunition in case we run into trouble and an extra barrel for the Browning …. Oh, and first aid kits, don't forget those."

"That should cook their goose."

"Ask Lakota to alert Browning as soon as we know this thing is a go."

"Is he in a safe place?"

"Yes. As soon as we wrap this up, we'll head for Virginia. Does that senator have someone lined up to take our place?"

"That's been taken care of. Senator Cruz has a bill in Congress to fund soup kitchens all over the country. It looks like Treasury would purchase distressed properties. Then farm them out to be renovated and managed by the military. It sounds pretty good if they can keep the bureaucrats in check."

"I hope it goes through. A lot of people are struggling to get back on their feet. Let me know if there's any change with Langley."

"I will. Be careful out there, Gunny."

"That's affirmative. So long, General."

KANDAHAR

"I have been studying online, Abdul, about victories of the Second World War and Vietnam."

"What victories, great one? I do not understand."

"Surprise and rapid deployment, those are key essentials for defeating an enemy."

"But for what end, Amir? Still, I do not understand."

"Think of the many Muslim tribes scattered around the Middle East and around Africa. They are our brothers. They hate the infidels just as much as we do."

"But they are small. We are no match for America or the Chinese."

"What if all of them became one holy army for Mohammad?"

"But how, Yusuf? It sounds like a dream."

"It is a dream, Abdul. The dream of Boko Haram, al-Qaeda, Islamic Jihad, Taliban, Hezbollah, and a hundred more. Together, we are the mighty warriors for Allah."

"But they're scattered and most of them lack financing. Some even fight among themselves. How would you ever bring them together?"

"There are hundreds of poppy fields in Afghanistan and thousands of other operations in the Middle East and Africa. What if every one of them contributed to a central bank? In a year's time we could raise a fortune."

"By the beard of the Holy Profit! Allah has given you a sign."

"Some will require weapons. Getting them organized into an army would take time and money. They would need food and shelter. And we would have to do this in secret as much as we could."

"It would take a year, maybe longer. You would have to meet with them and explain your plan. Maybe give a little money to get some of them back on their feet."

"Yes, the poor man lusts for money like the donkey lusts for the carrot. I think with enough money our army can become a reality."

"What is the goal, Yusuf? What will be our great objective?"

"Israel."

$10,000.00

Two weeks elapse. It was almost closing time when the Mercedes pulled up in the parking lot. El Diablo walked in by himself. His driver remained in the car. He and Gunny sat down at a rear table.

"I have a proposition for you."

"A proposition?"

When you unload your trucks, I want you to send them down to me in Mexico. I have merchandise to deliver in your country."

"Why don't you use your own trucks?"

"Border Patrol would arrest them. My merchandise is illegal."

"If it's illegal, what if I get caught? They could put me out of business."

"I'm prepared to offer you $5,000 a trip."

"A used rig these days costs $20,000. If they close this place down, I'm shit outta luck. I'll do it for $10,000."

"You're a hard businessman, Mister Buckner. I came with a packet of $5,000. I'll count out the rest. Here's 10Gs for the first truck and a map to my place with my cellphone number. Your driver will be given instructions once he's loaded. Instruct him to stop at the front gate."

"It's a pleasure doing business with you Mister Diablo. I look forward to a long and profitable relationship."

El Diablo left the building and his driver drove him away.

Once the last trays were in the dishwasher, James Buckner called his men together in the dining room.

"We hit the jackpot. El Diablo just gave me $10,000 for the use of our next truck. We'll be hauling dope for the cartel."

"Gunny, won't more Americans die from that shit?"

"Some may die, yes. What I didn't tell you before, the Vice President has a special task force for tracking these deliveries and arresting the American drug dealers after we hit the Mexican cartel. Congress doesn't know about this and may never know. We have a second assignment in Virginia once we finish down here. All of you will receive promotions and all of you will be sworn to secrecy. General Steele recommended each one of you. I think she did a hell of a job."

"Gunny, with all that money, can we get a second dishwasher? The one we have is kinda small."

"Sure thing, check it out."

"I have already, sir. There's a man in Del Rio closing his pizza joint and retiring. He has a good washer he'll sell for $350. Said he'd bring his plumber down and hook it up for free because of the good work we're doing."

"Tell him to come on down. Say, why don't we cook him and his plumber a special dinner?"

"How 'bout lobsters, sir? They's a place in town that sells seafood."

"Lemme see now, there's fourteen of us and two more makes sixteen. Get thirty-two lobsters. That's two apiece. What about pies? Is there a bakery in town?"

"There's a little mom-and-pop bakery. They got good stuff."

"Invite them out and ask them to bring samples. I want you people to judge. If you approve, we'll buy pies and cakes for our customers. I bet some of our kids never saw a pie or cake before."

"Gunny, you shouda been a dadjim preacher."

WASHINGTON, D.C.

"That is correct, sir. Contact has been established and the first bribe received. Gunny bought a second-hand dishwasher, and is buying pies and cakes for his customers. That man is a jewel, Mister Vice President."

"I wonder if he realizes how dangerous all this is?"

"He knows. I picked them special. They're all combat veterans. Kidwell, Browning, and Buckner served together during the war. Roy Jones is a sniper. He had over a hundred kills during the conflict. Buckner and Jones went to cooking school after it was all over. I asked them why they did that. Their responses were much the same. They wanted to forget the war."

"There will be no forgetting where they're going."

"They know, sir. These four men are all wedded together over the death of Browning's daughter. The CIA betrayed him to the cartel who kidnapped the girl. She was sold into the sex trades. Browning rescued her but it was too late. He placed her in a convent where she killed herself. These men want their pound of flesh, and I'm paving the way for them. I wish I could go too but I can't take the risk of getting killed. My position here is too important."

"Indeed it is. I need you for special assignments, General."

"The CIA has tried to nail Browning twice. He killed four of them last time they tried. When he discovered their connection to the cartel, they panicked. Those clowns have been going downhill ever since. It reminds me of the Kennedy assassination."

"We got rid of one herd of useful idiots now another one crops up."

"What's it like on Capitol Hill these days, sir?"

"Nothing like before the war, but we still have our share of political buffoons."

"Leftovers from the Generation X crowd?"

"I call them the Worst Generation. Bad parenting and Marxist professors ruined so many of those kids. But I don't blame the children so much as I blamed our Marxist government. They were brainwashed into believing that rubbish."

"Just be glad we won the war or you and I would be in a concentration camp or pushing up daisies."

"Let the men know I have their back."

"I will, sir. Its men like you and Senator Cruz that makes my job a labor of love. Getting rid of bad guys is something I wouldn't trade for anything. Thank you for letting me be a part of all this."

"Thank you for being there when I needed you. God speed, my friend."

"Goodbye, Mister Vice President."

LAKOTA KIDWELL

Gabrielle Browning and Mika Kidwell were having coffee and lemon cookies in General Steele's office. The General had baked the cookies the night before. They were waiting on Mika's husband, Lakota. Ten minutes later he arrived. General Steele served Lakota after he was seated.

"I have good news. Gunny Buckner has received a $10,000 bribe and one of our trucks is on the road to Mexico. So it appears our plan is underway. The Vice President has been informed. And all the weapons they need have been delivered. This may take a few weeks until the cartel gets accustomed to our trucks coming and going.

"Lakota, call John and ask him to come on in to the Island. Our soup kitchen is a big success."

"I never told anyone this before but it's one of many reasons why I respect those characters. All of us fought together during the war. Everywhere we went there were thousands of dead people and starving civilians. The stench was so bad you could almost touch it. Starving kids were the worst with their little tummies stuck out. There were atrocities too. In a small town in Alabama we came across a children's orphanage. The Progressives had been there before us. It was a slaughterhouse. After that we stopped taking prisoners. It affected James worse than the rest of us. He would wake up at night crying. Roy stuck by him like glue. We all did to keep him from killing himself. Some did, ya know. After a while he snapped out of it.

"When we heard about your daughter, Gabby, I overheard Roy talking to him one night. The war was over then. Roy told him, 'They have sewn the wind. Now they shall reap the whirlwind.' I was impressed by what he said so I looked it up. It's in the Bible, Hosea 8:7. After they came back from cooking school we swore an oath to avenge your daughter."

The meeting adjourned and Lakota went back to his quarters. Browning was radioed.

"It's a go. Come on in to P.I."

PIEDRAS NEGRAS, MEXICO

Highway 277 runs forty-seven miles between Crystal City, Texas, and Piedras Negras, Mexico. Piedras Negras is a central city for a mining and manufacturing community, an international highway, and a railroad and airport. El Diablo's compound is northeast of the downtown metro area.

"Did you see my little friend in the pool enclosure?"

"Si, *amigo*. The alligator, she must be twelve feet."

"Twelve feet and ten inches to be exact. I introduce him to those who displease me."

"Do many people displease you, El Diablo?"

"Very few since I acquired my pet."

"Does your pet have a name?"

"His name is El Demonio. That's Spanish for 'devil.'"

"You didn't send for us to admire your alligator. Why are we here?"

"Your commissar told me you are the best."

"We have killed many *gringos* and our kinsmen many times over."

"There is a man in Crystal City. I want you to bring him here to me."

"Does this man have accomplices?"

"He has thirteen accomplices. I want you to kill them all and bring him here.

"How will we find him?"

"I will give you the address. His name is Buckner. He is a big man with yellow hair."

"Why are you going to so much trouble over this man?"

"He dishonored Marko and he insulted my offer of $5,000 for the use of his trucks."

"How much do you have to pay?"

"He demanded $10,000 for each trip. I am not accustomed to being denied what I want."

"Transporting drugs is risky business. Ten thousand seems reasonable to me."

"That is none of your business. I make the decisions around here. You will do as you are told. I want this wrapped up in two or three weeks. That will give you enough time to execute a plan."

"I consider this operation questionable but you paid for it so we will do as you request. Then we're flying back to Cuba. We were warned you might be difficult. You are one strange *hombre*, El Diablo."

MIKA KIDWELL

Mika was lying in bed beside her husband with her arm behind his neck and her head resting on his chest. She is concerned over his upcoming trip to Mexico. It was dangerous and she knew it. Her doctoral thesis at The University of Tennessee was on The Trail of Tears where the Cherokees were assembled in Tennessee for their long and difficult journey to Oklahoma. Mika is Cherokee. So is Lakota.

"I love you, Lakota. I worry about your trip with Mister Browning."

"It will be a piece of cake. We'll be in and out in less than a day."

"Drug lords have hired guards. I do not want to walk my trail of tears all alone."

"Do you remember our first meeting at the clinic?"

"You came through the front door. I looked up and I knew immediately you were the one."

"You were wearing your cute little nurse's cap. I was struck by a lightning bolt. It was all I could do to ask your name. And you gave it to me, and your phone number."

"I gave you much more that night, didn't I, my love?"

"Making love with you is like a trip into the spirit world. I am a great warrior with a white stallion. You are my woman. We are free from all the lies and treachery of the white man. It's always that way with you."

"I'm happy you feel that way."

"I got a good one when I married you."

"You brought me to life as a woman."

"We have a good life together. Would you like to have a child, Mika?"

"I will give you anything you want. Anything you desire of me."

"Let us try to get you pregnant. Don't take your pill in the morning."

Mika sits up in bed and slips off her nightgown. Then she lies back down and positions herself underneath Lakota, her nipples firm and erect.

BAGHDAD

Abdul had assembled twenty-four clerics in a downtown mosque in Baghdad to listen to Yusuf's idea about the poppy fields, a central bank, and jihad against Israel. The guests were served unsweetened tea, dates, nuts, and pita bread with honey. The eldest among them was an eighty-two-year-old Grand Iman everyone referred to as Master.

"The Germans called it *Blitzkrieg*. They assembled their panzer tanks at a central point and smashed through the French defenses which were spread out over hundreds of miles. The French had better tanks and a larger army, but they were led by incompetent generals. France went down to defeat in six weeks."

"But we have no such army of tanks. Some, yes, but it would take thousands. The Jews have their Intelligence. So do the Americans and the Chinese. We would be caught out and slaughtered like goats in a pen."

"Have you forgotten the American 9/11 or the Tet Offensive? Or the 1973 Yom Kippur War? There was no warning. The Americans and the Israelites were caught off guard."

"Yes, but we have no great army, only small groups scattered over thousands of square miles. We have no satellites or aircraft carriers. We are small by comparison, even with the Jews and their military, which is very powerful."

"But what if we could combine our small forces all together into one mighty army?"

"How could we do such a thing? To begin with, it would cost a fortune. We would be spotted and the bombers would come. And where would you lodge them even if you raised such an army? The whole proposal sounds like madness."

"Turkey is 30% woodlands. Iran has the Hyrcanian Rain Forest which covers twenty-one square miles. The men could be moved at night and hidden during the daylight hours. In regions with no buildings or trees, we could move them a little at a time in small numbers."

"This would cost millions. Where would we find such riches?"

"Afghanistan produces 80% of the world's opium. Iran deals in large shipments of arms. Syria produces Captagon. Jordan, Lebanon, and Turkey have their amphetamine trade. Parts of Africa deal in human trafficking. Our Quran forbids all of these activities. Yet we Muslims do it for the money."

There was dead silence for a few moments. Then cursing and yelling. A chair sailed on to the stage. Dates were thrown at Yusuf. A glass bowl of nuts shattered on the stage floor. Shoes were thrown.

"Silence!" The Grand Iman commanded them to stop.

"I want to hear what this young man has to say."

"Thank you, Master. Every country in the Middle East and parts of Africa has their illicit trades. My idea is for each group or country to donate 25% of their income from those activities to a central bank I have established in Afghanistan. My income this year from the poppy farm will exceed $20,000,000. I pledge 25%. I estimate it will take a year to gather our army. We can hide them in the forests and villages. Israel is not a large country. When we are ready we can attack with a million men. Hanoi learned early in the Vietnam War to have their soldiers fight in close quarters. That way the Americans could not use their planes and artillery. I believe we can overrun Israel in one month."

"There is wisdom in your words, Yusuf, and much danger. Are you willing to try and bring the tribes together?"

"Abdul and I will dedicate our lives to Jihad. We can travel to the different places, but we would need support to convince the brothers we are sincere. Otherwise, they might think us charlatans trying to steal their wealth. They might even kill us."

"I will help you, Yusuf. I will send out my blessing to all the tribes. And I will support your 25%. If you can raise such a mighty army, our prayers of a hundred years will be answered. And that land inhabited by the Jews will once again belong to Allah."

TELAVIV

Netanyahu was asleep in bed. His staff had insisted that he get some rest. The man was exhausted. Looking after 10,000,000 Jewish citizens surrounded by five Arab countries, four of which were sworn enemies was an endless task. Netanyahu was eighty-one. Ethan, an aide, and Amos, a general, were enjoying a cold Goldstar beer in the command center's private office.

"Sir, the borders have been quiet for two weeks. Do you think we can relax a little while longer?"

"Maybe. You never can tell what the crazy things will do next."

"I remember when I was a boy my father used to tell me stories from the Bible: Samson and Delilah, David and Goliath. He was killed two years ago at the Syrian border. I wish I had the strength of Samson. I'd show those Syrians a thing or two."

"We have his strength, Ethan, and a thousand times over. If it ever appears we are about to be overrun we would employ our Samson Option."

"We cadets studied that in our military classes. The bomb dropped on Hiroshima was the equivalent of 15,000 tons of TNT. We have a wide variety of nuclear warheads, some are terrifying. They could level a large city."

"I hope it never comes to that. We Jews are hated around the world. I've never understood why. We're not aggressors. We're not colonialists. Yet people hate us. It makes no sense. If we use nuclear weapons to defend ourselves, we'll never hear the end of it."

"That's because most people are ignorant, sir. Muslims study one book, the Quran. India and China are well-read, but Americans for the most part are dumb as a box of hammers. They watch TV and read paperback novels."

"Yes, but the Americans are our friends. I'll take them any day, paperback novels and all."

"I meant no disrespect, sir. Winston Churchill saved the world against Adolf Hitler in 1940 and 1941. England fought the Germans alone for eleven months and twenty-eight days. Operation Sea Lion was called off in November 1940 because of Luftwaffe losses. Then the Americans entered the war in December 1941.

"Donald Trump saved the world in 2024 and 2025 against the Progressives. He and Field Marshal Feng went on to defeat the Marxists in China. Trump used nuclear weapons in China. For that, he was declared a hero. I guess we Jews are stuck with being black sheep."

"You're well-versed on your history, Ethan. Study the tactics Trump and the Field Marshal used against their adversaries. And study Vietnam. LBJ got them into that war then refused to let them win. He was a terrible commander-in-chief, much like Obama and Biden. It's believed Johnson was involved with several murders in Texas, including JFK. Obama may have been born in Kenya and not Hawaii. Joe Biden was a corrupt politician his entire career."

"How do you know all that about those presidents?"

"Trump shared FBI information with Bibi. Bibi passed it along to our general staff."

"I better wake him now. He said two hours."

"Give him another fifteen minutes. Bibi needs his rest."

STRANGERS

"Gunny, do you see anything different about those two men at the far table?"

"I don't know. What's bugging you?"

"The jacket that little guy has on is quality material."

"How do you know that?"

"My mother worked in a men's clothing store. My sister took me there when I was little. Mom and Julia talked about fabrics and men's fashions all the time. They sold good stuff there. That jacket the little dude is wearing is expensive. His buddy has on a pair of new shoes. They don't fit in."

"Take a tray over and see if you can hear anything."

Gunny went back into the kitchen and began slicing pies and cakes. He enjoyed watching the children's eyes when their mother or father placed a slice of pie or cake on their tray. He and Roy had finally found their inner peace.

Two days later another pair of men walked in wearing upscale attire.

Roy took a tray over and ate his meatloaf with mashed potatoes and gravy. The green beans were delicious, cooked in bacon grease. The cherry pie was fresh from the bakery. That evening after everything was put away, Roy and Gunny talked.

"Monday, I wasn't sure. Now I am. Somebody is casing the joint. They were speaking Spanish. I caught the word Cuba a couple of times. If they're from Cuba, what do you think that means?"

"I think we better alert the men and call the General. This could be trouble. Give the men their rifles and get my handgun for me."

Twenty minutes later Gunny had located General Steele at Parris Island.

"Roy got wise to them because of the clothing they wear. His mother worked in a men's clothing store. I'm not sure what's going on, but Roy is distributing the rifles as we speak. He thinks they may be from Cuba."

"I don't like the sounds of this. You have a flat roof. Post guards up there at night. I'll do some checking and see what I can find out. If the men have to go into town send them in pairs, armed. Stay frosty out there, Gunny."

JOHN BROWNING

Browning had just arrived at Parris Island. Lakota met him at the Greyhound platform. General Steele was waiting for them in her office.

"That's it in a nutshell, John. Some funny business is going on and I suspect that drug lord is behind it. I talked with Guantanamo. They know of special teams in Cuba that hire out, usually to kill someone, or help throw an election. Lakota has a squad of veterans on standby. Can you leave tomorrow morning?"

"If Gunny and his men are facing trouble, we better leave tonight."

"I don't know how serious this is but I don't want to take a chance. You and Lakota take the men down to armory and draw whatever you need. I'll notify the airfield to get a plane ready."

Midnight. Twelve Marines were airborne over Georgia on their way to Crystal City, Texas. General Steele radioed ahead to let Gunny know they were en route.

3 a.m. They were standing around the statue of Popeye the Sailor outside the air terminal. Roy and James pulled up in a school bus.

"Welcome to the spinach capitol of the world, jarheads. Climb onboard."

Cooper climbed in first. John and the others followed the dog. Lakota brought up the rear.

"Roy, I hear you and Gunny have become foster parents."

"I guess we have at that. The kids love us. We have desserts and coffee for you guys back at the cafeteria."

Roy drove to the soup kitchen and everyone unloaded their gear. Once the Marines had stacked their rifles they were served. John asked Gunny a question.

"What is going on over here? The General thinks Cuba is involved. She mentioned the cartel. If it is Cuba, it may be a team of assassins. But why would they be after the soup kitchen?"

"El Diablo has been bribing me for the use of our trucks at $10,000 a pop. I have nearly $48,000 in cash in my desk drawer. Maybe they're gonna rob our ass and steal one of our trucks."

"And maybe he's gonna kill ever body here."

"I never thought much about that but it makes sense. He thinks our trucks are not inspected at the border because of what we do here. Border Patrol was asked to stand down until the FBI could determine who the drug dealers are in our country. After that, we hit Diablo."

"Sounds like Diablo is about to hit you."

"We've waited a long time to nail that bastard for what he did to your daughter. We have twenty-six men here. Why don't we move our timetable up a week or two?"

"I think we better."

"There's a side road running off Highway 277 to a small fishing village behind El Diablo's compound. That side road is about a mile from the compound fence. They's about thirty Mexicans living there. I'll box up some food as a peace offering. Roy can run into town and buy a few tools and some fishing gear."

"Where we gonna sleep tonight?"

"There's an abandoned church just down the road. The men will have to sleep on the pews until I can buy some mattresses tomorrow. The heads are still operational. We have enough blankets here for everybody. You'll have to stay out of sight until we're ready to roll."

"When's the next truck goin' down?"

"We got another shipment coming in Thursday."

SHERIFF LONG

"Senator Cruz asked me to drop by and introduce myself."

"Come on in, Sheriff, and grab yourself a tray.

"That's right neighborly of ya … don't mind if I do. You ole boys are doin' a great job out here. Folks back in town are singing your praises."

"I'm proud of what we've accomplished here."

"I have three kids dead from fentanyl back in town. Ted told me why you're here. I would like to go with you when you shove off."

"Senator Cruz must have a lot of faith in you. You can't reveal this to anyone."

"Ted and I are old friends. It will never go beyond this room."

"Do you have any military experience?"

"I worked as a saboteur during the war with my friend, Carlos Antonio. We blew railroad tracks, bridges, you name it. Carlos is good with dynamite."

"Can Carlos keep his mouth shut?"

"He saved my life once when I was trapped with some of our men in Tennessee. He brought down a landslide on top of the enemy. He won't talk."

"I noticed your hands are calloused, even your fingertips. What caused that?"

Gunny laughed. "Roy notices everything about a person."

"I don't mind your asking. I'm helping build a new schoolhouse. Progressives burned our old one. They burned our courthouse too."

"Is this Carlos person available?"

"Carlos is my deputy."

"We may need dynamite. You think so, Roy?"

"I believe we will. Welcome onboard, Sheriff. Bring Carlos with you. Do you have vests back at the jail?"

"I imagine we have the same things you have, Roy. And enough dynamite to blow Mister Diablo and his Mescaleros into the next county."

"Bring Carlos out for lunch tomorrow. We'll introduce you both after we close."

The next day Carlos and Sheriff Long arrived just as the last customers were leaving. They were treated to Gunny's special spaghetti recipe with all the trimmings. Afterwards, they were introduced. Carlos caused a stir among the Marines.

Six feet tall, black hair, black eyes, dark complexion, one hundred and seventy pounds. His uniform was immaculate, brown Stetson hat, and spit-shined black boots. The holster he wore was black patent leather, holding a six-shot .44 magnum.

The sheriff spoke softly to Carlos. "Tell them how we met."

"My name is Carlos Tupac Antonio. My father was Kickapoo. My mother was African American. They died during the war. I met Sheriff Long at Eagle Pass. I joined his team fighting the Progressives. In a battle outside Del Rio we captured a trainload of dynamite. Sheriff Long and I became very good at blowing up Progressives. They put a price on our heads so we slipped into their camp one night and blew up their headquarters. It is an honor to work with you Marines. El Diablo needs killing."

Gunny stood up and welcomed the two men. Then Sheriff Long spoke.

"Drug traffic is coming across the border by every means you can imagine—private planes, trucks and cars, even the rail lines. We catch a few but the majority slip through. Diablo is behind all this. Carlos and I will assist you any way we can. We have Browning automatic rifles and bulletproof vests back at the station house. We'll be ready to go when you are."

LIGHTS OUT

Later that night, after Lights Out, Mississippi was talking with Michael Cohen from New Jersey.

"I been thinkin' about that alligator."

"You gonna catch it and keep 'im for a pet?"

"No, I been studin' on how somebody can be that cruel.

"My major was psychology before I quit school and joined the Corps. Some kids are born bad, it's like they got no sense of right and wrong. Some switch is turned off in their heads. Others get that way from being raised by unstable parents. And some are just plain crazy. Diablo sounds like a psycho to me."

"You think he's crazy?"

"Part fruitcake, part asshole."

"What did you think about Carlos?"

"I'd hate to meet him some night in a dark alley. Did you notice his eyes?"

"Not really. What do you mean?"

"When I shook his hand he looked me in the face. It felt like he was looking inside me. It was like he was reading my mind."

"I read something about that once. They say some people can see the future."

"We better get some sleep. Six o'clock will be here before ya know it."

SYRIA

The meeting place was in a large temple on the bank of the Barada River west of downtown Damascus. Numerous groups were represented, including Ansar al-Islam, the Abdullah Azzam Brigade, Abu Sayyaf Group, al-Mulathamun Battalion, and al-Qaeda from five different regions. Yusuf walked out to the podium and tapped his microphone to see if it was on. A hush fell over the audience.

"Peace be upon you, my Muslim brothers!

"The Master sent each one of your leaders an invitation to come to this meeting. I am Yusuf Aziz, your ambassador for a greater Islam. Our goal is to raise a great army for jihad. Our target is Jewish Israel. Beyond Israel lies Western Europe. Our victorious ancestors …"

"Stop! Stop right there." A chieftain from Hezbollah was on his feet. "You talk like a fanatic. This has been tried many times and always with the same result, humiliation and defeat. Your words are those of a lunatic."

"You speak the truth, my brother, but we were never united before. Always before, we fought with small armies. We never united together as one army."

One of the Houthis rose. "Let him speak. I have not heard this before."

"Thank you, my brother. The plan is to unite the tribes under one flag like Muhammad did when he founded Islam in 610. Such a mighty force could crush Israel in weeks. Do not be afraid of their atomic weapons. If we rush in among them, they will not bomb their own people. This was proven in Vietnam at the battle of the Ia Drang Valley in 1965 when the communist PAVN engaged the American Army and almost defeated them."

"But how could we ever accomplish such a thing? Our fighters are spread out in many corners of the East. We would be attacked by the Jews and the Americans once they discovered our presence."

"We travel only at night. In the daytime we remain hidden. All of this can be coordinated among the tribes. It will take time and wealth, but we have that wealth among us."

"Among us? What do you mean, among us?"

"Each clan will contribute 25% of their annual income for the cause. The Master has already given his 25%, and so have I. So have others. It is a small thing when you consider what will be gained. Elimination of the Jews, and a return of that land to Allah."

"But will the Americans bomb us if we succeed?"

"Not if we take hostages, at least one thousand. The Americans covet life. They will bend over backwards to get those hostages back. We can eliminate most of them while keeping a few dozen for show. By the time they realize what we've done we will have infiltrated Western Europe. We will slay infidels by the millions. Those of us who die shall live on in Paradise."

A great discussion took place among the guests. This went on for half an hour while Yusuf and Abdul waited nervously seated on the stage. They knew what was decided would make or break the dream.

Finally, a chieftain from one of the al-Qaeda clans rose and motioned for silence.

"We have talked among ourselves and we want to know where the 25% is to be held and who will control this great wealth? Who will be responsible for its distribution, and how will we know if it is being rationed wisely?"

"Excellent questions. I found a bank in Kandahar I trust which will keep our secret. I invite you to choose four clerics among yourselves to work with me and the bank. That five will make the decisions on how to spend the funds wisely. The Master chose this number. With five there can never be equal disagreements."

Another discussion took place. Ten minutes later the same chieftain rose again.

"Who will decide the time and place for the attack?"

"My thoughts are, leave that to the Master. If you prefer to do that yourselves, let the elders of our tribes decide. My suggestion is to attack all four sides at the same time. That would weaken their forces."

This time the discussion was brief.

"It is agreed among us that 25% shall be the price of victory. The date for our attack the Master must decide. May Allah be with us in this our holy crusade against the Jewish infidels."

WASHINGTON, D. C.

"Do you believe it's that serious?"

"Yes, Mister Vice President. Guantanamo reports a group of mercenaries left the island a week ago. I believe those are the men in El Diablo's camp. If that's the case, our boys are in harm's way."

"You've alerted them with your findings?"

"Yes, Mister Vice President. I've spoken with James three times over the past twenty-four hours. Browning and our men from Parris Island are there now. The operation has been moved up ten days. Senator Cruz and the Rangers have been notified."

"Please call me Victor. All this formality is a waste of words."

"I wonder if we should alert the Border Patrol?"

"I wouldn't do that. They may have an embedded mole."

"Do you think we should change our plan and try and take Diablo alive?"

"After what you told me about that alligator, they should hang the son of a bitch."

"Did Senator Cruz get his soup kitchen bill through the Senate?"

"Indeed he did, with a strong bipartisan support. Democrats today are nothing like the ones we had with Obama and the Biden Administrations. They care about the people and they care about our country. President DeSantis is like that. He works tirelessly helping the people get back on their feet."

"I've often wondered why so many of those bygone politicians turned crooked once elected."

"Washington is a town of intrigue and temptation. Power and money are intoxicating influences. Over the years it became the way of doing business until Washington was totally corrupt. Obama used that weakness to promote his agenda against the Republic. Senator McConnell was little more than a rubber stamp. It took a civil war to break the cycle."

"We came close to losing our Republic, didn't we?"

"If the Progressives had won, we'd be like Cuba or the old Soviet Union. Until President Trump used those B-52s, the fight could have gone either way."

"Drugs are another corrupting influence. They steal a person's self-will."

"Yes, but we've got a cure for that in Crystal City."

"I'll be in touch as soon as they move out, Victor."

"Goodbye, my friend."

CHRISTMAS EVE

The soup kitchen was packed with people standing in line around the room. Gunny had prepared fourteen turkeys and eighty pounds of cornbread dressing. Beans, corn, okra, mashed potatoes, and cranberry sauce were stacked in the kitchen beside dozens of pies and cakes. Out front, in the center of the dining room, stood a nine-foot Christmas tree. The people were celebrating the Christmas spirit. And sitting among them was the captain of the Cuban assassination squad. He had come for one final assessment of his contract with El Diablo. A little girl sitting beside him asked the man a question.

"Do you know about Santa Claus? My mama said he has eight reindeer that can fly. Mama said he will come tonight and leave a present for me. He didn't come last Christmas because mama said his reindeers got sick."

"Your mama was right. Santa's reindeer were sick, but this year they're on the way."

"Do you think it will be something nice like a baby doll or some new shoes, maybe? My shoes have holes in the bottom and my feet get wet when it rains."

"Did you tell your mama what you wanted for Christmas?"

'Oh, yes. I told mama I wanted God to thank these men for giving us good things to eat. Daddy used to be tired a lot and he got sick a lot too. Now he's all better and he goes to work every day."

The little girl turned to her tray of food and began to eat. The assassin turned his attention to the big man with yellow hair standing against the rear wall behind the serving counter. He stood up and walked toward Gunny. Roy had been watching the man and moved closer with his .45.

"Are you Mister Buckner?"

"Yes sir, what can I do for you?"

"I'm Sabastian. I was hired to kill you and your team."

Roy moved in beside the man, his automatic stuck in the man's ribs.

"Don't be alarmed. I mean you no harm. I was raised Catholic by my mother. What I see here is one of God's blessings. I will not honor the Cuban contract with El Diablo."

"Why are you telling us this?"

"I do not wish to go back there. I will tell you his evil plans. Can you hide me?"

Roy turned the man to face him, looking him in the eyes. "He's telling the truth, Gunny."

"Roy, take him back to the church where the others are staying. When the crowd clears out, bring everyone back here. We'll decide then how to go about this."

Three hours later, twenty-four Marines and Sabastian were seated in the dining hall with Roy and Gunny serving them. Sabastian stood up, explaining the plan he had put together for El Diablo.

"My not being there won't stop them. They will think I'm in jail or dead. Counting Diablo's men, there are forty-one of them. The plan was to surround this building at 5 a.m. on New Year's Day. Then order you to come outside. We did not know you were Marines, and we didn't know about the church behind here. We were going to kill everyone except Mister Buckner. El Diablo wants him for his alligator.

"I am ashamed to have been involved in such a scheme. We didn't know what it was until we got here. Nevertheless, I told Diablo I would honor the contract. What you've done here has turned my world upside down. If I go back to Cuba, I will be shot. I wish to stay here with you people."

Roy set down a full tray at Sabastian's place at the table.

"You're welcome to stay here with us. We'll decide how we're going to deal with that degenerate across the river. You can help out with the meals."

The next day Sabastian had finished wiping off tables when he noticed the same little girl who had spoken with him the day before. He went over to pick up her tray. Sabastian looked down at the child who had fallen asleep with her arms folded and her head on the table. His mind drifted back to another December 25th when his mother told him that Christmas was the darkest day of the year. Why? He asked. She explained that Christ was the light of the world and the Romans had crucified him. He pulled out a roll from his sport jacket, peeled off a hundred-dollar bill, and stuffed it in her tiny plastic purse. A feeling of warmth descended over the man, starting at the top of his head and flowing down. He felt nostalgia over his childhood. Sabastian wondered if he had just been touched by an angel.

MEXICO

El Diablo was furious. The intended date for the attack was five days away and the captain of the hit squad was missing. Two squad members had attempted on two occasions to investigate the soup kitchen but each time they found Texas Rangers parked in the parking lot. They reported back to El Diablo that it appeared Sabastian had been taken into custody. The next day they made a third attempt. The Rangers ran their car off the road and arrested them.

El Diablo flew into a rage when they failed to return, screaming and cursing.

"YOU IDIOTS ARE SUPPOSED TO BE PROFESSIONALS! PROFESSIONALS, MY ASS! SEBASTIAN IS GONE! NOW, TWO MORE HAVE DISAPPEARED! I AM NOT ACCUSTOMED TO NOT GETTING WHAT I WANT! AND WHAT I WANT, WHAT I DEMAND,

IS BUCKNER BEGGING FOR HIS LIFE AT MY FEET BEFORE I FEED HIM TO El DEMONIO!"

"But, *Senor*, Sabastian may be dead. We must show proper respect."

"FUCK RESPECT! FUCK HIM! AND FUCK YOU! I PAID $200,000 FOR THIS STUPID CIRCUS ACT. GODDAMMIT, DO SOMETHING!"

"Please, *Senor*. Do you want us to go on with the contract?"

"YES! YES! *ESO ES SUFICIENTE*! Now get the hell out of my sight."

That night the Cuban mercenaries met in the squad bay of the barracks building. They were disturbed over their leader's absence and angry with Diablo's disrespect. Miguel was especially put out with their employer.

"*Ay caramba*, Mister Big Shot Pendejo is a man too big for his pants. First, he insults Sabastian. Then, he insults us. He is *que fula*. We should stuff him in that cage with his alligator."

"You have the good idea, Miguel. But we are under contract. We would all be in trouble if we kill this foolish man."

"That is true, Manuel. But I would very much like to see him with his alligator."

"Enough of this. With Sabastian gone and those others missing, there are seventeen of us. Diablo's men number twenty-two. Some of them will stay behind with El Diablo. We can expect maybe ten. Put them in the middle of the caravan so none of them can slip away. We may need their guns if the *gringos* fight.

"Juan, you will lead the caravan. Bembe, you bring up the rear. Remember, park out of sight in case they have sentries. Then we slip in and surround the building. I will bring the bullhorn. When they come out, line them up against the building. Save the big one called Buckner for our full-of-shit employer."

VALLEY OF THE GUN

Highway 227 has a narrow divide through a low series of hills a few miles south after crossing the bridge over the Rio Grande River. It was there the Marines chose to spring their ambush. The idea was to place railroad ties across the highway so the Cubans would be forced to stop. They would then be ordered to lay down their weapons and surrender.

NEW YEAR'S DAY, 4:05 a.m.

"You see anything yet?"

Gunny Buckner was standing on a flat rock looking down the highway with a pair of night binoculars. "Not a damn thing, Roy. They're due right now according to our Cuban friend."

"Give it time. They'll be along."

"I see headlights. A bunch of 'em. Get those railroad ties out."

Several railroad ties were spread in the road to look as if they had fallen off a truck. Rolls of tarpaper were placed among the heavy timbers. The convoy stopped. Several men got out to clear the highway. Back at the bridge, the Texas Rangers had set up a roadblock.

"You are surrounded. Lay down your weapons. We do not intend to harm you. Put your hands in the air. You are surrounded. Lay down your weapons. You will not be harmed."

A firefight erupted. Men were shot dead. Gunny stood up to call a ceasefire. He was struck by three bullets, two against his bulletproof vest and one through his shoulder.

"You idiots stop firing or we will kill every fucking one of you sons a bitches!"

The firing slowed and stopped.

"Medic! Medic!"

"Gunny, you got a hole in your shoulder."

"Gimme a shot. Call the ambulances. Call the sheriff. Tell 'im to bring Carlos. Now get down there and help those fuckers. Take some men and go with Doc. Stick that boy with an arm wound before you go."

Down on the highway, the situation was grim. Eight men were dead. Three were dying. The medic didn't bother with them. They would die anyway. Eleven men were wounded. Five were uninjured. Doc hurried among the wounded doing what he could to help the worst ones. Then the sheriff and Carlos arrived. Carlos brought a Mexican priest with them. The priest knelt with the dying, giving them the last rites. Carlos went among the injured, talking to them in a calm voice and giving them water from his canteen. Two ambulances drove up, loaded three men apiece, and drove for the hospital. Those less injured were loaded in trucks and followed the ambulances. The sheriff and Carlos took the five captives back to the jailhouse. There they were given hot coffee and BLT sandwiches from a café down the street, and locked up.

Doctors and nurses were called in from all over Crystal City. Gunny was still in surgery when the wounded began arriving. A call went out over the local radio station for blood donors. When it was learned the soup kitchen was involved, citizens flocked to the emergency room.

Back on the highway, Marines and Texas Rangers were clearing away the wreckage. The dead were piled in two pickup trucks and taken to the morgue. City wreckers were busy with the damaged vehicles. Four of the trucks were still operational so the Rangers drove them to the holding facility behind the jail.

7:42 a.m. The Marines arrived back at the soup kitchen, tired and dirty. A group of people were standing in the parking lot, asking what happened to breakfast. Roy began to laugh. So did Mississippi and the rest of the crew.

"Come on in everybody and take a seat. We'll have your breakfast ready in a few minutes."

TEXAS RANGERS

January 3rd. Captain Smith with the Texas Rangers was in conference at the soup kitchen with Roy and his Marines. Carlos was present. The sheriff was in town minding the jail. Diablo's compound was under discussion. Gunny Buckner was still in the hospital.

"The outbuildings are no problem but that house is built like a fortress. I drove by there last week. We were told to stay away because we have no jurisdiction in Mexico. You Marines are just what the doctor ordered."

"How big is the place?"

"Sixty acres but the house sits within 200 feet of the driveway. I saw two guards on the front gate."

"He's down ten guns from our highway fight. If Sabastian is right, he's got twelve guns left, thirteen counting himself."

"We better assume he knows we're coming."

"If I was Diablo I would expect a night attack. So I suggest we go in the middle of the day. We can see better then anyway."

"I agree. We can spot anyone trying to get away too. We'll serve lunch then hit the bastards around three o'clock. That may catch 'em with their pants down."

"Carlos, how much dynamite you got?"

"I will bring two boxes. That should be enough."

"Okay, we're goin' Sunday."

"John, go into town and get ten gallons of kerosene. Lakota, you go with him."

"Frank, your arm ain't well. You stay here with the dog and mind the store. We should be back around dark."

"Captain, bring your men over at twelve o'clock Sunday. We'll eat then shove off."

Three days come and go. The Rangers delivered a five-ton flatbed with a fourteen-inch I-beam for a front bumper. The tripod for the .50 caliber machine gun was mounted on the wooden deck of the truck. Sandbags were stacked in a circle around the gun for protection against small arms fire. The pickup trucks were loaded and parked out back. Dawn came on a cold and windy morning. The Texas Rangers arrived and everyone ate lunch.

"I don't like the looks of that sky. It's blowing up a storm."

By the time the Marines and Rangers headed out, the wind had picked up considerably. Daylight began to fade as the storm intensified.

"This shit is getting serious. You think it's a twister, Captain?"

"I don't believe we've ever had one in January. It's just another storm off the Gulf."

"Well, what the hell is that thing out yonder?"

The captain laughed. "That's a dust devil, Roy. We get 'em all the time here in Texas."

Carlos: "This storm is a good omen. They won't expect us in this."

When they crossed the bridge, whitecaps were breaking on the river below. Leaves and tumbleweeds were blowing across the highway. Lightning spider-webbed the horizon. It seemed to Carlos that his ancestors were smiling down on them.

They stopped a hundred yards from the front gates. Captain Smith pulled out his field binoculars.

"It's locked. This rig will make short work of that."

They hit the front gate at 40 miles an hour. The chain snapped and the two metal gates flew in opposite directions. Bad Boy halted the flatbed beside the concrete walkway. The troop transport and the pickups pulled up on the far side of the flatbed. John and Lakota manned the machine gun. Carlos ran for the end of the building with a box of dynamite. The Marines and the Rangers spread out in a semicircle.

"You are surrounded. Lay down your weapons and come out. Send the women out first. You have two minutes. Your friends are all dead or in jail. Send the women out now."

A minute passed. Seven females came running down the sidewalk. They were instructed to go down to the entrance and shelter there. Automatic fire began coming from the windows. The .50 caliber opened up, blowing the front door to pieces. Twenty-seven men poured a withering barrage into the building. Carlos set his fifty-pound box against the end of the building, lit the fuse, and ran. He was struck and fell. Roy ran out to help his friend. He was hit in the vest while dragging Carlos back into the trees.

Roy yelled over to John.

"Get that sumbitch in the rear window."

Fifty-caliber slugs walked across the building, blowing out the glass and part of the window frame. Fire continued coming from the opening. John lowered his elevation one click. The windowsill disappeared in a cloud of splinters, along with the top of the gunman's head.

The explosion blew off the end of the structure.

"That shooter got me. I'm done for."

"I'll go find Doc. I'll be back in a few minutes."

"... no ... stay with me ... I don't want to do this alone ..."

"Doc can fix you up. I'll be back in ten minutes."

"... my fixing days are over ... please ... stay with me ..."

Roy took Carlos in his arms and held him.

"I'm here old friend. I won't let go."

"... I can feel it now ... it's not like what they say ... the shadows are closing in ..."

"God be with you, Carlos."

"... there's a light up ahead ... I can see it ... I can see ... it's ..."

Carlos passed over to the land of his ancestors. Roy sat holding his friend with tears spilling down his cheeks.

"So long, ole buddy ... Save me a place at the table."

Gunfire continued for another ten minutes. Finally, only sporadic shots were coming from the windows. The Marines rushed the front entrance. One man rose up to fight and was shot dead. A wounded man at the middle window raised his rifle and he was killed. They found El Diablo lying on a couch with a bloody shoulder wound.

"So, you dirty *Gringos* have beaten my *solados*. But you have not beaten El Diablo. Do you think I am so stupid I have not prepared for a day such as this one?"

"Why don't you tell us about it, Mister Diablo?"

"I am El Diablo, the great one. I have important friends in many places, but I will not tell you. You can't kill me. You would be much in trouble with your superiors. Yes! You people are nothing. You're peons, order-takers, little people, nobodies."

"Are you referring to your friend in the State Department? No? Perhaps those bought and paid for colonels over at the Pentagon? Or maybe you meant your crooked legal associate at the Justice Department? They can't help your sorry ass, *amigo*. They've all been arrested for treason."

"That is no matter, I have millions. I will make you rich. Take me to the hospital. I have rights."

"Yes, you do, Mister Diablo. You have the right to an execution."

"No! Stop! I am El Diablo! I am the chosen one. You have no legal right to harm me. I demand ..."

Roy handed John his .45. John walked forward and shot El Diablo between the eyes.

It felt as though a weight had been lifted. He had finally avenged the death of his daughter. The blood oath was half complete.

"Check the house for valuables. See if any money is lying around. That painting up there on the wall is a Picasso. Wrap that in a blanket and put it in the truck. Take down those swords and pistols. They look like they might date back to the Conquistadors. That coffee table is a work of art. General Steele will love this stuff in her office.

"Guys, you better come look at this."

In a bedroom with no furniture, bundles of hundred-dollar bills were stacked three feet high, wall-to-wall.

"Search the kitchen for trash bags. Check the outbuildings, anything that will hold this money, pillowcases, sacks, wooden crates. The General is gonna flip out when she sees this!"

"Sir, that building out back has kilos of cocaine stacked to the ceiling. And big jars of pills on the shelves. You think we should put the dynamite in there?"

"Good idea. The blast should destroy a lot of that shit."

With the house and barracks going up in flames, they stopped at the front gate to gather up the females. The explosion blew two tons of cocaine and thousands of pills into a gray winter sky.

A cold wind was still blowing when they pulled onto the parking lot back at the soup kitchen. A medical team was waiting. The body of Carlos was brought in and placed on a table. Gunny met them at the front door.

"What's the damage, Roy?"

"We lost Carlos. Two men are wounded, nothing too serious. The Rangers lost one man and one man wounded. He's hurt but he'll live. We have seven women outside in the truck, and about a thousand pounds of hundred-dollar bills. I left Diablo and the dead men inside the house. We set the whole place on fire, and we blew up his lab full of cocaine and pills. The 'gator is still there."

"Bring the ladies inside, we'll feed them. Where did the Rangers go?"

"They took their man to the hospital in town."

"Call and ask if they can get these ladies home. They're better acquainted with the territory. And bring that money inside and stow it in the gun room."

The sheriff was notified to come and take Carlos back to town. He cried when they laid him in the truck bed and covered him with a blanket. Money changed hands for his funeral, the town, and for the Kickapoo school where Carlos taught Indian History.

Captain Smith drove over for the women. Gunny counted out a stack of money for the dead trooper's family and $150.000 for their retirement fund. That evening the Master Sergeant brought out two quarts of Wild Turkey to celebrate the end of the drug cartel. The next morning it was business as usual, feeding poor people and making kids smile.

KANDAHAR

"I can't believe so much money has come in so quickly. Already we have two hundred thousand men waiting in the forests in Turkey. At this rate, we can be ready in five or six months."

"You are a genius, Yusuf. You optimize a second coming."

"No, Abdul. Mohammad received Allah's Commandments. We are Allah's disciples for *Jihad*."

"Then let us go forth among the kingdoms and claim our destiny."

"Yes, Abdul. The time has come for our journey. The Great One has prepared the way. Now we must finish the task."

"The railway system is limited. We can rent a bus and camels where no roads exist. In the mountains it is cold at night. We must take warm clothing, Yusuf."

"I think it would be most wise if we buy a bus. We can take everything we need, including signs for our meetings. Good slogans are essential. We can take turns driving and we can sleep on the bus."

A fortnight passed and they were ready. *Za'atar manouche* for breakfast, and they were on their way. Before them lay an arduous journey and an uncertain date with destiny. That first day, they spent the night in Kabul where a group of one thousand had gathered to hear Yusuf speak. There were skeptics in the crowd.

"... it has been tried before and always with the same end. Defeat, bloodshed, and shame. Why is this time different? And why should we trust you? You ask for men and gold. What is your experience in warfare?"

"Mohammad was a shepherd and a merchant yet he established Islam with only 313 followers. In the Six-Day War, Nasser lost his entire air force on the ground. Yasser Arafat was such a thief and liar that he made things worse for Lebanon and Palestine."

"Words, just words. What gives you the right?"

"The Master gave his blessing and his 25%. Are you prepared to do less?"

An angry stir went through the crowd.

"Sit down, Big Mouth. Sit Down And Shut Up! We want to hear what he has to say."

"Thank you, my brothers. Thank you. Our goal is to raise a force of one million men and two hundred million dollars. We will attack Israel from all sides then rush in among them. That way they can't use their planes and artillery against us without killing their own people.

"The forests in Iran and Turkey will hide the majority of our holy warriors until we are ready. We have five trustees overseeing the funds flowing into the bank in Kandahar. We estimate Israel can be overrun in a matter of weeks."

"When do you foresee the approaching battle?"

"It will take Abdul and I another six to eight weeks to cover all the Middle East. Volunteers and money are pouring in at an astonishing rate. We estimate June or July. Our volunteers travel only at night. Most spy satellites are not equipped with night vision. Some are, but we know those flight patterns. This must remain our secret until all is in readiness."

"Will many of our young men be killed?"

"I won't lie to you. We estimate 15% to 20% casualties and perhaps that many wounded. Death is not our enemy. Paradise awaits those who fall in battle."

"Will you be going with our warriors?"

"Abdul and I plan to be in the front ranks."

Another stir went through the assembly, this time with emotion and animated conversations. Yusuf and Abdul sat quietly at their table onstage, eating dates and sipping unsweetened tea.

"A hundred and fifty to two hundred thousand is a high price to pay. We have doubts. Our sons could be among the dead."

"There are 10,000,000 Jews in Israel. If we kill them all, we'll be getting fifty of them for every one of ours. In past battles these odds were reversed, and we never won a war. The Jews always prevailed. This way our sacrifice will be for the extermination of the godless infidels and the land will return to Palestine and will once again belong to Allah."

A powerful chieftain of Hezbollah arose, brandishing a pistol for quiet.

"I say a vote is in order. Those among you who agree with these two gentlemen onstage, raise your hands."

A sea of hands went up.

"It is settled then. We are with you. Tell us where to send our money and the places for our volunteers to hide. In my village, we have over seven thousand young men and much silver."

Names and addresses were exchanged and Yusuf and Abdul retired for the evening. They slept in their bus with a small heater attached to a drop cord to keep them warm. Bathroom facilities were available in the building beside their vehicle.

ROY

"James, what happened when you blew a fuse at the orphanage? What did you think? How did you feel?"

"That's a hell of a thing to ask. I don't like talking about it."

"I have my reasons ... please, I need to know."

"Is something bugging you?"

"It's personal ... I can't ... it's ... I feel like ..."

"You feel like what?"

"I think there's something wrong with me."

"Why do you think so, Roy?"

"In my dreams … In my dreams, I'm always lost. I can't find the car … I'm on foot. I'm trying to go home … but I'm miles from home … sometimes in a rough part of town. And every time I wake up I'm sad … and sometimes it makes me cry."

"Okay, I'll tell you. I felt like there was no God … my world died with those dead children. I was overwhelmed with all the death we'd seen. When I saw those little bodies, brains on the floor, blood splattered all over the walls … my mind zoned away to Crazy Land. That's when I wanted to kill myself."

"I know, James. I never left you alone until you snapped out of it."

"Trying to go home sounds like something to do with your family. Did you get along with your mother and father?"

"Part of the time. I was raised a spoiled brat."

"They must have loved you if they spoiled you."

"We never talked much about important things. They came up hard so they let me go my own way. They came from the Old School so they didn't know how to reach me. I never had discipline until I joined the Corps. The Marines saved me from what I was."

"You grew up as a child so you did childish things. Is that about right?"

"My father died when I was young. Mom and I were at the hospital. I remember standing beside his bed holding his hand. I wanted to say 'I love you' so bad I couldn't stand it. But I couldn't get the words out. That's how locked up I was inside."

"Only a man can admit he was wrong."

"I was a punk-ass kid with a convertible and a boat. He paid my college too."

"It's pretty obvious why you're having those dreams. You want to tell your daddy you love him."

Roy began to cry. "I want to go home and see my mama and daddy."

"You are home, my friend. The Marine Corps is your home. Someday you'll see your mother and father again."

"After our promise is kept with John, I don't want to shoot people anymore."

"I'll speak to the General. We're trained chefs and good ones too. When we get back to P.I. with all that cash in the back room, she'll let us do whatever we want. She likes you, Roy. You have a proud service record. We both do. After Langley, we'll hang up our shootin' irons and concentrate on feeding our Marines."

"I'm glad we serve together, Gunny. It makes me proud to call you my friend."

MASHHAD, IRAN

A cellphone call was received from an elder in Mashhad urging them to come at once. The drive took twenty-one hours. When they arrived at the designated location, three elders ushered them into a small warehouse. Sitting near the warehouse door was an oblong wooden crate with a metal control panel attached to the top of the box.

"The Great One gave us your number and told us about your mission. We asked his advice because of what we have here. We don't know what to do with it."

"Are you talking about that box?"

"Yes, it's a nuclear warhead."

"You can't be serious!"

"It's a 200-kilogram warhead off a damaged BrahMos missile. Comrade Putin shipped two BrahMos missiles before Tehran was destroyed. We found this one a month ago in an underground bunker. An electrical genius from the university built this. It can be armed in three stages."

"By the beard of Allah! This is a miracle."

"The bomb weighs 440 pounds. The crate with the batteries and all the wiring weighs 488 pounds. We want you to take it with you for the crusade."

"How does it work?"

"To arm the bomb you pull out this titanium rod on top of the box. This is thirty-four inches long. You discard that. Then you set your timer. These numbers, one through nine, represent hours. When the timer reaches zero the bomb will explode. To start the countdown, push the red button.

"The engineer told us that if it's going to be hauled, place it over the rear axle. That way the steering won't be affected."

"We've already taken out the last two rows of seats to make room for our mattresses. One more row will place the box over the axle. Bring a toolbox and we'll get started."

An hour later the warhead was loaded with a forklift and secured against the rear seats. Yusuf and Abdul bedded down for the night, sleeping with the bomb between them. Dawn came early. They ate flatbread and honey with the elders and went back on the road.

BIRJAND

When they reached the outskirts of the Iranian city, they were greeted by a police escort that led them back to the mayor's office where the mayor was waiting with the director of public security and the city elders. Master had called ahead, instructing that they be treated as honored guests. A small banquet was prepared, fish steak with garlic and mustard sauce, buttered chicken, sweetbreads, and pickled peaches. Afterward, Yusuf explained his plan for holy warriors and the 25%.

"We have gold left here by the Germans. They came after the Russians crossed into Poland. Our grandfathers told us. They were afraid because they were on the side of Germany. They believed the Americans would come and bomb us but they never did."

"Where do you keep your gold?"

"It's 12 kilometers north of here in a cave. We never go there because of the evil spirits."

"What evil spirits?"

"The Germans killed their laborers, who were Russian prisoners, so they could never return and steal the gold. It is an unholy place, my brothers."

"Will you show us the way?"

"I will take you there but I will not go inside."

An hour later they were standing before a cave entrance at the base of a mountain range. Thousands of bones littered the landscape. Bits of olive green uniforms and leather boots lay about. Skulls lay among the snake plants and desert scrub.

"This is an unholy place, Yusuf. Must we go inside?"

"If there is gold in there, this could be the answer to our prayers. Come, and bring those flashlights."

Inside the entrance, the ceiling rose up into an antechamber which led to a much larger room beyond the beams of their flashlights. They could see gray mounds covered with tarpaulins in the distance. The cave was dry and musty.

"I do not like this place, Yusuf. It has the presence of the grave."

"Come now, Abdul. Do not be a fraidy cat. I want to see what those big piles are."

Yusuf pulled a tarpaulin off the first mound he came to.

"Look, Abdul, look! Boxes of rifles. We can use these."

He uncovered mound after mound, exposing hundreds of boxes. Then he found machine guns and mortars and tons of ammunition. There were medical supplies and an x-ray machine. Finally, he came to the last four mounds at the rear of the chamber.

"Gold, Abdul, stacks of gold. Four pallets of gold! One of these ingots weighs about twenty pounds. Gold is worth \$2,500 an ounce so one ingot has 16 ounces times 20 pounds. That comes to ... 320 ounces. Three hundred and twenty times \$2,500 ... \$800,000 for one ingot, Abdul! Each pallet has 20 across and 20 lengthwise. That comes to 400 times 20 stacked ingots equals 8,000 to a pallet. Eight thousand times four equals 32,000 bars of gold. Two thousand five hundred multiplied by 32,000 ... I'll have to work this out.

"Eighty million, Abdul, and with all these weapons we have here about one hundred million in gold and guns. I will call the Ayatollah and tell him we need trucks, an army of trucks. This makes our mission much easier now.

Let's take a couple of these pistols to protect ourselves and some gold bars. We might need those too. We can hide the gold under the front seats."

"I'm glad we're leaving, Yusuf. This is a terrible place."

HOHENFELS, GERMANY

"Sir, I'm getting something on the satellite radar that doesn't make sense. Right there, can you see it?"

"I saw it but it just went away. What is it?"

"The satellite signal indicates it's radioactive. What you saw just passed out of range."

"That doesn't make sense. The only thing radioactive in Iran is the ruins in Tehran."

"I saw it this morning, sir. But I waited to tell you until I got a second reading. Whatever it is has moved fifty miles since 11:44 a.m."

"It's probably a simple explanation but keep an eye on it. If it pops up again, call me."

One hour and ten minutes pass.

"Sir, I've got it again. It appears to be moving west."

"Get on the horn and call Offutt in Nebraska. Explain the situation. Ask them to put a satellite on Iran."

It took six minutes to get through to Offutt.

"Captain Carroll asked me to call. We have something on the screen here that suggests it's nuclear. It's on the ground and it's moving."

"When did you notice it and where is it?"

"11:44 a.m. our time. Birjand, Iran. Since then it's moved west close to eighty miles."

"Do you have any idea what you're looking at?"

"We don't know, Colonel, but it's giving off a faint signal."

"It's probably nothing but we'll take a look. We'll have another set of eyes in that region in half an hour. I'll call you back as soon as we know something,"

Forty-five minutes later.

"Is this Sergeant Brooks?"

"Yes, sir."

"We pulled up a school bus. Whatever is giving off that signal is on that bus. We believe it should be checked out. Mossad has assets in the region. Call them. Highway 68 is a secondary highway. He just passed Tabas on his way toward Poshi-e Badam. Mossad will know the area."

ELIJAH AND SAMUEL

The Mossad team was parked on the side of the highway watching for school buses. So far they had inspected only one, with negative results.

"We sure get some crazy assignments. A radioactive school bus! Next, they'll have us inspecting outhouses for atomic bombs."

"Well, least ways we're not getting shot at like our border patrol back home."

"Yeah, those poor guys draw the short straw every day. We should blow those assholes away and be done with it. World opinion is an old maid sob sister. We should have finished off Hamas and the Houthis when we had the chance."

"Hey, look, there's another one. And that old boy is loaded. See how the backend is low with the rear tires?"

The four-door sedan pulls up behind the school bus, flashing their lights. Yusuf pulls to the side of the highway with the Mossad vehicle pulling in behind him.

"Abdul, when I open the door you step down and shoot them. Pull the hammer back. It makes it easier to fire."

"You in there ... Step outside, please."

Abdul stepped down on the lower step, raised the P38, and shot Elijah twice in the chest. He turned to Samuel and shot him three times. Elijah fell dead with a bullet through the heart. Samuel stumbled sideways, tumbling down an embankment.

"Roll that one down the bank. Now, check the bomb to see if it's still covered up."

"I found the problem, Yusuf. One of the lead aprons slid off. I will weigh them down with our gold bars."

Yusuf calls the Great One for advice. Ayatollah Akbar instructs him to turn around and go to Kandahar. Yusuf turns the bus around and heads for home. In the meantime, the Ayatollah floods the highway with school buses.

"This is Samuel Green. Elijah is dead. I've been shot. That school bus ... probably ... has a bomb. Send an ambulance ... I'm ... I'm passing out ... "

GENERAL STEELE

"The men over at the armory spent ten hours counting the drug money. The total is $49,920,400. That Picasso you brought back is valued at $90,000,000. Offers have come in from all over the world. The Vice President said, sell it. They'll use the money for our soup kitchens. Same deal with all that cash. He said keep some for whatever we need here. I'll put that in the bank and send the rest to Washington. Victor Hanson and Senator Cruz can handle that end.

"Roy, I understand you don't want any more combat assignments."

"Yes, Ma'am. After I fulfill my promise to John, I'm done with wasting bad guys. I just can't do it anymore. Carlos was the last straw. He died in my arms."

"Gunny thinks the world of you. So do I, Roy. Do you want a discharge?"

"No, Ma'am. I want to be a chef right here on the Island."

"I was hoping you would say that. Gunny wants the same thing. The two of you will make a great team in the mess hall. When are you guys leaving for Langley?"

"Next Tuesday. There'll be only one guard on the front desk that day. The staff will be away on a training exercise."

"Be careful. I don't want to read about my people on the front page of *The New York Times*."

MISTER ASSHOLE

Traffic was heavy on the George Washington Parkway. To make matters worse, they were in the midst of a thunderstorm. There was a wreck up ahead so they were creeping along at 5 mph toward their exit. Finally, they got off and parked in one of the visitors' parking spaces near the front entrance.

"Remember, five minutes. Let's go."

A uniformed guard was seated behind the reception desk wearing a 9mm Beretta.

"We want to go to the sixth floor."

"Do you have a pass?"

"No, you're going to take us."

He reached for his pistol. Four revolvers appeared, pointed at his face.

"That's a silencer in case you've never seen one. The .38 won't make much noise but people may hear you scream when I shoot you in the foot. I know the alarm so keep your hand away from it. That button there locks the front door. Push it! Now, turn off the cameras. Lakota, go hang your TEMPORARILY OUT OF ORDER sign. Son, left hand, put your shiny new gun in the desk drawer."

In the elevator, John asked the young man a question.

"Is Martha still on the desk upstairs?"

"Yes, sir."

"Martha's a good egg. She won't give us any trouble."

"Hello, Martha."

"Holy Shit! I thought you were dead."

"That'll be the day. Is Mister Asshole still at the end of the hall?"

"Mister Asshole is still there. And just as full of shit as ever. You here to kill 'im?"

"It crossed my mind."

"There's a dickhead from Blackrock across the hall from Mister Asshole. He's trouble. Here, use my passkey. Larry, these men are good guys so stand easy. Go over there and sit down."

At the end of the hallway, they opened the Blackrock door first.

"Who tha fuck are you?"

He reached for his gun. Four silencers made their debut. Next, they opened the door across the hallway.

"Hello, Mister Asshole."

"John! I can explain. It wasn't my fault. I swear ..."

John shot him in the forehead.

"He keeps the key to that wall safe in his vest pocket. Open that sucker up."

"Looks like a hundred and ten grand in packets and a batch of legal documents."

"Use the waste can. Get it all. Let's go."

Back out front at Martha's desk:

"Larry hated the bastard like the rest of us. Tell us how to play this."

"Four strangers came in wearing COVID masks. They made me lock the door and turn off the cameras. Then they forced me onto the elevator. Up here, they threatened Martha and used her passkey. Then they left and I pressed the alarm."

"Practice telling your story before you call the cops. There was $110,000 in his safe. Martha, you have seniority so you get $60,000. Larry, here's $50,000 for you. Keep this money at home. No banks. Spend it wisely. The Feds may be watching. Larry, give us two minutes before you hit the alarm."

"My lips are sealed, fellas. Thank you for this wonderful gift. And good luck."

"Goodbye, John. Come see me some time."

"God bless you, Martha. You too, Larry."

Downstairs they pushed the release button, retrieved their plastic sign, and walked to their automobile. They were pulling onto the Parkway when they heard the alarm.

WHITE HOUSE

"That's right, General. We don't know any more than you do. The Chief Inspector with the FBI is working on it. He hasn't come up with anything yet.

"I'm no good with guessing games. I have no idea who would want to kill our CIA Director.

"I'll keep you and the Joint Chiefs in the loop. We're just as concerned as you and the Pentagon. This was an attack on our democracy."

"Good health to you, Mister President."

"Thank you. I wish the same to you, sir."

"How'd I sound?"

"Very convincing, Mister President. He bought it."

"I'm glad you told me about the drug cartel. Common sense tells me the Director was involved, but I don't want to know anything about that or the people involved. That way I don't have to lie to the press or take a chance on exposing the good guys."

"How do you like my soup kitchen program?"

"Victor, you amaze me. I would never have thought of something like this. And here you and your team are, buying up bankruptcies to feed the poor. You've put a feather in all our caps."

"I got the idea from a soup kitchen we set up in Texas. It was such a success it made me and some others realize how strong the need is to help poor people get a decent meal. There's still a lot of pain and misery out there from our Civil War and the men who caused it."

"That honor falls in the lap of Barack Hussein Obama. Joe Biden was a political sideshow. President Obama was a communist plant that fooled everybody."

"Well, he sure fooled me. I never trusted the man but I never realized how awful he was."

"Columbia University has a sister school in Moscow. One of our visiting professors spotted Obama on their campus. We suspect that's where he trained, and studied the Cloward-Piven Strategy. Then Soros and Schwab brought him over here as a graduate from Columbia in New York City. Hillary was squeezed out and the Democrats made him president."

"I believe if it hadn't been for President Trump, we would have lost our Republic."

"Are the people involved with that CIA Director and the drug cartel out of harm's way? By that, I mean is there any chance they'll be found out?"

"None that I know of, Mister President. I think we're home free in that regard."

"I certainly hope so. I'd hate to get caught up in a flap like President Nixon."

PARRIS ISLAND

"Thank you for agreeing to see me, General Steele. I have a question to ask about one of your Marines."

"Has one of my men done something wrong?"

"I believe John Browning killed the CIA Director."

She paused, shaken, collecting her thoughts.

"What in the world gave you that impression?"

"A film I picked up at Langley headquarters. I studied the pictures then I superimposed a photo I have of John Browning on the film. Even wearing a COVID mask, the image was unmistakable."

"Has anyone else seen this imaging?"

"No one, only myself."

"Why did you come here to accuse Captain Browning?"

"Curiosity. Ego. You see, I'm good at what I do. I just want to know if I'm right."

"Why would I give up one of my Marines to satisfy your curiosity?"

"You already have when you looked away when I mentioned John's name. I've been schooled in human responses. Your reaction was a 'tell,' just like poker."

"Are you going to bring suit against Browning? If you do, I will fight you with the finest lawyers money can buy. Your dirty laundry will be hung out for the whole world to see."

"Don't get all het up on me, General. I came here as a friend of the Marine Corps. In this briefcase are all the papers I have on Browning. The Langley film is in there, plus John's photograph. I'm leaving this with you and writing off my investigation as a dead-end. I'll make note that the murder might have been retribution for a past conviction."

"Mister Smith, may I invite you to dine with me in our mess hall? We have a couple of excellent chefs."

RENDEZVOUS

"Hey, mister, got a light?"

"Sure thing. Here, let me light your cigarette."

"Come with me. I have some people who want to meet you."

The stranger led Mister Smith down an alleyway. When they rounded a corner there stood three men warming their hands over a fire in an oil drum.

"Hello, Mister Smith. My name is John Browning. These fellows are my accomplices."

"I hope you didn't bring me back here to kill me."

"On the contrary, sir. There's a Pancake House a block from here. Would you care to join us?"

After finishing their pancakes, Inspector Smith was let in on the whole operation.

"We operated out of a soup kitchen in Crystal City. El Diablo was about as bad as they come. We killed him and burned his compound to the ground. The alligator went to the zoo in Mexico City. Then we snuffed the Director and that bastard from Blackrock. General Steel told us what you did so we brought you a gift to show our appreciation."

Each man pulled a Krystal bag out of his coat pocket and slid them across the table.

"There's a packet of hundred-dollar bills in each bag. The General wanted you to have this. Not as a bribe, but as a token of our friendship."

The inspector placed the bags inside his coat pockets.

"In a courtroom this might be construed as a bribe. Coming from the four bravest men I ever met, I consider this a patriotic honor. Thank you so much. Now I can get that new washing machine my wife has been asking about."

Everyone laughed.

"Gunny and Roy are retiring from the field. Lakota and I will be available if you ever need our services. It's been a pleasure meeting with you, Mister Smith."

"Likewise, Mister Browning. Take my card. If you ever confront a situation you can't get a handle on, give me a call. I have contacts all over the country that help with my investigations. No one ever need know I'm involved with you Marines."

MOSSAD

"Elijah was shot dead. Samuel is in the hospital. Before he went into surgery Samuel said he thought the school bus has a bomb. Germany picked up a radioactive signal then it stopped. Offutt had the bus on satellite and lost it when about twenty other buses showed up. Those other buses were sent there to stop us from looking inside that school bus. I believe Samuel was right. It could be a dirty bomb, or it might be something worse."

"Do we know where it came from?"

"No! It was headed southwest then it turned around and went east on Highway 68."

"Anything new on weapons shipments?"

"Not yet. We're searching back ten years."

"This is a hell of a note. That school bus could be anywhere."

"Call in your markers. Find the damn thing."

Two frustrating hours drag by. The men and women assigned to finding the school bus know that the survival of their country may hang in the balance. They also know if a bomb was on the school bus it could have been transferred to another means of transportation. A message came in from U.S. Central Command.

"Here it is. I think the Americans found it.

"Two BrahMos missiles were shipped to Tehran by Putin's Russia before Tehran was blown off the map. A BrahMos will not fit in a school bus but the warhead will. It weighs 440 pounds and carries at least ten pounds of U-239. Kill radius is two miles. Destruction radius is four miles. Tel Aviv is twenty square miles. Something of this nature is too horrible to imagine.

"Find it. You are cleared to use any means necessary."

KARL AND LYDIA

Karl Goldman, trained as a human lie detector, was addressing his partner, Lydia Sams. Lydia is twenty-five, beautiful, and hard as tempered steel. Lydia has killed before. She admires Karl more than she lets on. The feeling is mutual. Lydia calls him her "Mind Reader." Karl calls her his "Iron Lady."

"I think we should go to Tabas and try to get some idea of why the school bus turned around and where it might have been going. What do you think?"

"I know why it turned around. They had been discovered. My guess is, they headed for home. That's what I would do. Go where I feel safe. Wouldn't you?"

"That's why we're partners. You see the obvious that I overlook."

"Come on, let's get to the airport."

From Tabas Airport, they drove by motorcar and parked in the parking lot of the Azadi Elementary School. There the two of them sat cogitating over what direction they might have taken with a nuclear weapon onboard. After a few minutes, they took the street up to Moallem Square then turned right toward Afghanistan.

Afghanistan was a long shot. Five miles out of Tabas, they stopped at a filling station, asking if anyone had seen a school bus. Their excuse was that their son had left his backpack onboard. Fifteen miles later, they made their third stop at a diner.

"Why yes, a school bus was here this morning. Two gentlemen came in and ate breakfast."

"Were they dressed in school attire or civilian clothing?"

"The tall one wore a sheepskin coat. The skinny one had on a leather jacket. They were very nice. They even left a tip. A lot of people don't leave tips since all the war trouble."

"Thank you, ma'am."

Lydia handed the waitress a five-pound note. They proceeded on, stopping every twenty miles to make certain they were still on the trail. Driving into Delaram, Lydia yelled, "Stop!" Sitting on the left side of the highway in a used car lot sat a yellow school bus.

"It can't be this easy."

"Come on, we have to check it out."

"Good afternoon. What can I do for you good people?"

"We're looking to buy a school bus."

"I just changed the oil and air filter. It came in this morning. Good condition. 117,000 miles. Tires are in good shape. I don't have a title. The driver asked for $1,500. I gave him $600 with no proof of ownership. But don't worry. I can make one up for you."

"Do you mind if we look it over?"

"Go right ahead. I'll wait right here for you."

Back at their Jeep Cherokee, they picked up a Geiger counter. When Lydia reached the back of the bus the device began clicking.

"We found the damn thing. Let's ask if he knows where they went."

"They're up the road about three miles at that motor lodge. Some friends of theirs came and unloaded the bus. It took five men to get a big box loaded onto a truck."

"What kind of truck was it?"

"It was one of those olive-drab army trucks. Say, are you interested? I'll let you have it for $700."

"We want to speak to the owner first. We'll be back."

Dusk was falling when they arrived at the motor lodge. A glance at the registry revealed four rooms were occupied. Three did not apply, but the name Yusuf Aziz stood out. They made their way past the soft drinks machine and the ice maker to the last room at the rear of the stucco structure. Lydia was sliding a plastic card inside the door lock when they heard gravel crunch behind them. She turned quickly with her .357 drawn. There was a flash and two loud reports.

Karl cried out grabbing his chest, collapsing to the pavement. A bullet struck her shoulder. Lydia got off three rounds, stumbling over backward. She hit her head hard on the concrete and lay there, stunned. The shooter disappeared. A door opened. Two men fled down the sidewalk.

"Lydia ... Lydia ..."

Karl's arm fell across her chest. Her vision began to clear. Lydia crawled over, sliding her arm beneath Karl's neck. She pressed her body against Karl. She knew the dangers associated with shock.

"The ambulance is on the way, lady. There's a dead man out in the courtyard."

"Bring us a blanket, please."

"Lydia ..."

"I'm here, Karl."

"I'm very fond of you, Lydia."

"This is a hell of a time to be expressing emotions."

"If I'm going to die, I want you to know."

"You're not going to die. The bullet missed your heart and it missed your lungs. You'll be out of the hospital in a week"

"Are you angry with me?"

"No, *Ahuv*. I've cared about you ever since you carried me away from that gunfight in South Africa. I was hurt so bad I didn't know it was you. Isaac told me."

"You never told me."

"I didn't want to give you a heart attack."

"Don't make me laugh. It hurts. I love you, Lydia. I want you to be my wife."

Lydia snuggled closer to Karl, smiling, and passed out from blood loss.

ABDUL AHMED

"It was a miracle that we escaped, Yusuf. Our guard, he was killed."

"It is Allah's will that we escape. Our destiny has been foretold among the stars."

"It must be true, Amir. They had us but we got away. Our poor guard gave his life for us."

"He is in Paradise. Perhaps even now he is gazing upon the holy face of Mohammad."

"There is a town in Iraq we should visit, Baghdad. There is much wealth and many warriors there."

"What tribes are present?"

"The Abu Nidal Brigade and the PLO."

"Excellent! They have fierce warriors. The trucks, are they hidden in a safe place?"

"Master directed us to a warehouse near the airport. It is heavily guarded night and day. The gold bars are there. And all the guns and ammunition. I disposed of our weapons in case we are stopped and searched."

"That was good thinking, Abdul. We don't need weapons anymore."

"Let us find another school bus. We can load everything we need and be on our way."

"I'm glad we're rid of that bomb. The thing made me nervous."

"I too did not like the bomb. At times I felt like it was watching us."

"Perhaps there is a demon inside that wooden crate."

"The bomb the Anglos dropped on Tehran devoured five million people. Let us hope the bomb we have at the warehouse is just as hungry for Jewish blood."

"Come, Yusuf. We must find a suitable school bus."

"Let's try the high schools. They have many buses. A small one would be easier to drive."

At the Kandahar Institute High School, they purchased an eighteen-seat school bus for $2,850. Yusuf thought it perfect compared to the twenty-four-seat vehicle he had been driving. They returned to their quarters and loaded their belongings. The trip to Baghdad was 1,246 miles and took them two days. In a large mosque, Yusuf spoke before a crowd of five thousand. There was order and respect. They knew of the success he and

Abdul were experiencing. Master had called to assure them and to ask for their support.

"So far we've gathered three-quarters of the finances necessary and now we need only 250,000 more warriors to fill our ranks. Warriors for *jihad*! Warriors for the annihilation of Israel! We are so close to glorious victory it steals my breath away. It makes me want to sing and dance in the streets. And with Abu Nidal and the PLO with us, HOW CAN WE FAIL?"

Cheers went up, the clapping of hands and the stamping of feet ... Abdul led the chant ... "Allahu akbar ... Allahu Akbar ... ALLAHU AKBAR!"

MESS HALL

Gunny was standing in the middle of the kitchen at Parris Island. He was admiring the space and all the appliances compared to the soup kitchen at Crystal City. Roy was standing beside him, grinning ear to ear.

"Isn't this wonderful? This is what we wanted. No more killing. No more shooting young men. I feel like I've been let out of some terrible prison. I haven't dreamed anymore about being lost either. You were right, James. I'll see my mother and father again someday. Do you have something special planned for dinner?"

"Why don't we make some tomato pudding? And all the usual vegetables and green beans cooked in bacon grease. And steak. There must be 500 pounds in the cooler. Sweet potatoes with brown sugar. Spaghetti with that special sauce you like. Baked apples, sliced tomatoes, and cucumbers. French toast, and peach cobbler."

"Damn, Gunny. You'll have the whole Island marching in those Fat Man platoons."

"Right on, my lad. Get those cooks crankin'. We got hungry Marines to feed."

General Steele had come over from her office to see how her two chefs were getting along their first week back.

"How you doin', Roy? What's good tonight?"

"I'm sure happy to be here, ma'am. Gunny Buckner is too. Let me fix your plate. Where ya sittin'?"

"I'm over there with John and Lakota. Mika is with us."

Roy brought over a steaming tray of spaghetti, steak, green beans, and tomato pudding. Milk was on the table. He went back and brought her a bowl of peach cobbler. General Steele was concerned over the news from Israel via the Vice President, but tonight she keeps that to herself.

"This tomato pudding is delicious. The steak is tender and Gunny's spaghetti is the best I've ever tasted. James and Roy could find work with any kitchen in the country. We're lucky to have them."

Lakota: "Those two guys are as lethal as they come. They have a knack for it. But killing people takes away your humanity. You descend into a dark world. All of us went there. Then Gunny blew a fuse and the rest of us weren't far behind. I believe El Diablo and that CIA creep freed us from ourselves. Those were righteous missions and they were good for the country. I'm happy to see Roy and Gunny with smiles on their faces again."

"They wanted to be in the kitchen so I put them in charge. Judging from this excellent dinner, I done good!"

Mika laughed. "Yes, you did, General. They're as happy as two pigs in a mud hole."

John asked a question. "Have you heard anything back from Mister Smith?"

"He called Friday and thanked us for his gift. He said his wife was beside herself with a new washing machine. He said to call him if we ever need anything. I like that man."

"It's hard to believe we got him as our investigator. Someone else would have turned us in."

"I took his briefcase down to the incinerator and burned it. I stood and watched to make sure the whole thing burned. We have nothing more to worry about with Mister Smith protecting us. The Vice President sent his congratulations."

"We should thank our lucky stars we know those people, and Senator Cruz and the Texas Rangers."

"Yes, and that sheriff in Crystal City. I think about Carlos a lot lately. He was a fine individual."

"Why don't we invite him to come and visit sometime? We could do something special to honor Carlos."

"That's a great idea. We could ask the chief of his tribe too."

Gunny came over and sat down. "What do you think of my tomato pudding? I think it turned out real tasty. I got the right amount of sugar this time."

"I thought it was awful!"

"What?"

"Just teasing, Gunny. It was perfect."

"You shouldn't do that to an old veteran like me. You could give me a heart attack."

"It'll take more than that, Gunny. You're one of the Old Breed."

"Yeah, remember that time in Chattanooga?"

"I'll never forget that one. We were trapped and you led us down to the riverbank and we got away in the dark."

"Then the damn boat sank out in the middle of the river. If it hadn't been for those seat cushions our asses woulda drowned."

"It don't matter how we did it, we got away."

"I wonder how Miss Martha's getting along. We could invite her to our shindig for Carlos."

"You think the Feds might be watching?"

"We can ask Detective Smith to check it out. We could invite him too if the coast is clear.

General Steele: "I don't think you should invite them. That's too much exposure. Let sleeping dogs lie."

Gunny: "I was thinking the same thing. Martha and Smith form a connection. If they came here, a smart investigator might figure things out. That would put us all in a 9 by 12 cell."

"You're both right. Carlos was our friend. We could ask the sheriff and the tribal council."

"Yes, that would be fitting."

"We have a new weapon at the armory that seeks out enemy troops. It's a shoulder-fired heat-seeking rocket that bursts over an enemy formation.

It's similar to a cluster bomb only smaller. There's going to be a demonstration at the range this Saturday at 10 a.m. I want you three to be there."

"Ten a.m., right, General. We'll be there."

CAIRO

Yusuf and Abdul were lodged by the elders in an ancient temple once inhabited by the pharaohs. Abdul is uncomfortable with their lavish accommodations. Yusuf is intrigued by them but he too feels out of place.

"I don't like it here, Yusuf. This is a place of sin. We could become corrupted. We should go back to our school bus."

"We can't do that. The elders would be insulted. We're here to raise money and get more warriors, remember? And besides, the food is the best we've ever had."

"I know, Yusuf. One could become addicted to such a lifestyle. That would defeat the whole purpose of our journey."

"You're right, of course, but I love the tender meats cooked in honey and garlic, and the pastries. Never have I tasted such delicious pastries."

"I don't believe Allah would approve of this place. We should get out as soon as your speech is over and the addresses given to the elders. Our souls could be in jeopardy."

"We'll leave tomorrow. In the meantime, I'm going to order some more of their delicious food."

The next morning at ten o'clock a fundraising rally was held in a vast temple with 25,000 eager participants. Word had spread among the tribes. The destruction of Israel was like a drug drawing them in. Muslims far and wide believed the hour of redemption is near.

Wealth flowed into the Kandahar bank. And the ranks of the warriors was almost complete.

"So you see, my brothers. With just a few more pieces of gold and a few more men, the Master will unleash our forces when the time is favorable. Even now, they wait in readiness, surrounding Israel. Three days' march by night will deliver the Jews into our hands. No mercy, my brothers. We must kill them all, women and children, so they can never rise again. Hitler showed us the way in *Mein Kampf*. We shall finish the task he started.

"There are tents along the way. Forests to hide in and whole villages have moved away making room for our warriors. There are stockpiles of food and water, rifles and machine guns, tons of ammunition and medical supplies. Victory awaits our brave soldiers. Paradise awaits those who fall in battle.

"Dig deep, my brothers. Bring your young men to the hiding places. You are among the last Abdul and I will visit. Soon we shall return to Kandahar to help with our troop movements. Those farthest away from Israel will start their journey first. Those closest to Israel will begin last."

Ten days later, all was nearing readiness.

NETANYAHU

"Something is going on. Intelligence can't get a handle on it so I've called on Lydia and Karl. They speak the languages and they know the people. Samuel is not well enough to travel and his partner was killed. I'm counting on Karl and Lydia. They left two days ago."

SECRET REVEALED

"Is something wrong, Karl?"

"You would have made a great slave driver on one of those Roman warships."

"Seriously, do you want to stop and rest a while?"

"Just a few minutes, Sweetheart. I've been shot before, but it never made me weak like this. It pisses me off, slowing us down so much."

"Take all the time you need, my love. Tonight I will rub your back and snuggle up beside you."

"I look forward to the day we can make love. The doctor warned me to refrain until the damage in my chest heals. That hollow point really did a number on my behind."

"I don't mind waiting. They put me back together with metal screws. This mystery is our baby. Poor Elijah is gone and the rest are out searching. We must find Bibi an answer."

"There's a restaurant up ahead. Let's stop and get something to eat."

Lydia had on dull conservative attire with a veil covering her face. Karl was wearing Muslim clothing and a black and gold Kufi hat. Upon entering the restaurant, they were escorted to a booth beside a window. They ordered lemon garlic chicken with chickpea pilaf and Russian tea.

"The food these people eat is good. I like it as well as our kosher dishes."

"Careful there, Karl. Next thing I know you'll be growing a beard. This chicken is tender and quite tasty. I wonder how they do this?"

"Stainless steel mallets. I saw it in a cookbook."

"We should get one for our steaks."

Waitress: "Are you going to the rally tonight?"

Lydia: "Ali was planning on going but we lost our directions."

"Four miles up the road there's a railroad sign. Turn left at that sign, cross over the tracks, and you'll see the mosque up ahead. It's only a few hundred yards from the railroad tracks. You can't miss it."

At the designated hour, Lydia waited in the car with her .357 in her lap. Karl went inside and sat on a rear bench. For an hour he listened to the usual mumbo jumbo and the great wonders of Allah and how superior he was over Buddha, Jehovah, and all the other deities. Then a bombshell landed at Karl's feet.

"When you leave tonight there's a wooden box at the rear exit for contributions. There's also a tear-off booklet with the name and address for volunteers. Be generous, and take one. Call the number on your tear-off for assigning young warriors. Master tells us the time is almost right for our attack against Israel. Safe journey, my brothers. Allahu Akbar!"

Karl contributed forty dollars on his way out and took a tear-off.

MOSSAD

"It appears we're up to our ass in alligators. Karl attended a meeting in Egypt where the speaker spoke of war with Israel. There was talk, asking for contributions and volunteers. We called a number Karl gave us but it shut down when it recognized our prefix. We tried again from across the border but the number was dead. If these meetings are taking place around the Middle East, we're facing a serious confrontation. I've alerted our armed forces and I've called President DeSantis. It isn't clear what we're facing so I've asked the President to stand by."

"Did Karl get any idea of how big this might be?"

"No, but Germany and America have been alerted to concentrate their spy satellites on the Middle East. A nuclear weapon may be in play."

"How deep are our stockpiles of ammunition?"

"Seven or eight weeks. After that, we would ask Germany, Japan, and the United States for assistance."

"What about Australia."

"I called yesterday. They're low on everything following the Civil War, but they do have two Battle Axe cruisers to patrol the Red Sea. The United States has dispatched two carrier groups for the Mediterranean. And Great Britain is sending the Queen Elizabeth. We'll have ample airpower."

"Sir, I suggest we place our Reserves on standby."

"I discussed that with Staff. They want to wait until the situation reveals itself. The economy will suffer if we pull them away from their jobs too soon. Let's wait and make sure our people have everything they need in case of a prolonged war."

"We should inspect our front lines. Make sure the men have everything they need."

"Good idea. Get started on that in the morning. Make sure our tankers have enough ammunition. The same is true for the gun crews. Check the trenches, water buffalos, fuel trucks, everything."

"Bibi, the IDF is sending drones out as we speak. If something is out there, we'll find it."

"Good! I want everybody to keep their cell phones handy until we figure out what we're dealing with. A few minutes can mean the difference between victory and defeat. Get enough sleep, eat right. I want all of you to be 110%."

ISTANBUL

Yusuf and Abdul were wrapping up their campaign. They had visited thirty-seven cities, had raised $153,000,000, plus $80,000,000 in Nazi gold. Volunteers number 931,000. This was determined to be sufficient by the Master. He wants the attack to begin before the hottest months of summer. Today, they are at an outdoor rally at the soccer stadium in Istanbul.

The stadium boasts a searing capacity of 74,735 and is full to standing room only. Abdul and Yusuf are on a wooden platform in the middle of a field with the mayor and the general of the Turkish army. The platform is surrounded by military police.

"This is our last stop before we head back to Kandahar to do the work of Allah. Glorious victory awaits us on yon horizon. Soon there will be no more Israel and no more kosher Jews. Palestine will be sponged clean of Jews and their profit Jesus Christ. Their temples will be torn down and the bodies stacked and burned until nothing remains but ashes. The land beside the sea once again will belong to Allah."

"When do we start? When do we march on the Jews?"

"Possibly within the month. Master will decide."

"Are you going with them?"

"Abdul and I will be in the front ranks."

"How many holy warriors do you have?"

"Over 900,000. The Master believes that will be enough."

"Some of us want to go. How can we manage that?"

"There are boxes out front for contributions. And paper tear-offs. Your tear-off will explain everything."

"Should we bring guns?"

"Holy warriors will be assigned to specified locations. Bring your Quran and toilet articles. Everything else will be provided, including weapons. If you have a favorite weapon, bring that with you. Travel only at night. Sometimes there will be trucks. Other times you must walk. Field commanders will instruct you on cooking fires and the importance of staying hidden during daylight hours. Do as the field commanders tell you. They are there for your protection and to maintain secrecy."

That night Yusuf and Abdul counted the day's proceeds.

"We did well today, Yusuf. There is a small fortune here. And many more volunteers. Master will be pleased with us."

"It seems like only yesterday when we started. We have come far, Abdul. A blessed event for Allah and Mohammad."

"Soon columns of smoke will be rising over Israel. That will be the culmination of Arab dreams. Do you think we will survive, Yusuf?"

"Allah will decide if we must die. We'll have our seventy-two virgins in Paradise."

"I want to live long enough to see Islam cleansed of the filthy Jews."

"That too is my desire. I want to see Israel lying prostrate among the ruins of history."

"Come, we must get this money onboard the bus. And also those boxes of pastries. I hope you aren't disappointed with me, Abdul. They're so good I asked for some to take with us."

"I could never be disappointed with you, Yusuf, and all we've accomplished. You have a sweet tooth. That is nothing to be ashamed about. I like the pastries too."

PARRIS ISLAND

Netanyahu had telephoned the White House twice in the past three days expressing his concerns over war. The borders were quiet, which was unusual. IDF drones had detected no ground movement, but excessive wood smoke was detected above the forests, north and south of Israel.

President DeSantis asked Victor Hanson to get in touch with General Steele. The President was impressed with General Steele and her Marines. She called in John and Lakota and her two chefs. Colonel Le Quire was summoned and so was Captain Rodriguez. All had served with guerrilla units during the Civil War.

"Netanyahu has a situation on his hands and the President asked us for an opinion. The Israeli border is quiet as a mouse but an unusual amount of smoke has been detected in the trees around Israel. The Prime Minister indicates that much smoke has never happened before."

"It sounds like a bivouac, General. They're waiting on something."

"I believe the Colonel is right. There may be an army of bad guys in there."

"A lot of smoke indicates cooking fires. I think Israel should prepare for the worst."

"Sometimes Intelligence is asleep at the wheel. Tet was like that, the Easter Offensive, and our own 9/11."

"Assuming that's the case, what do we tell the President?"

"Good question. We don't have enough facts."

"Something unusual is in there. Ask the IDF to try flying their drones inside the trees."

VOLUNTEERS

The IDF had already lost two drones that got tangled in tree branches. A third drone was sent in three feet above the forest floor. It hit a tree. Two more drones went in and disappeared.

General Steele was speaking.

"Drones have been tried and they failed. Israel appears to be surrounded. Victor Hanson believes Israel is facing another war. So does the Israeli Prime Minister. President DeSantis suggested sending Marines to patrol Tel Aviv and the IDF Command Center.

"DeSantis requested volunteers.

"Roy, I want you and Gunny to go with them. You'll be there to assist the Colonel and to run the mess hall. Rodriguez, stick with John and Lakota. If there's a breach in the lines, you three will gather a force to plug the gap. Be careful. The last thing you want is to be captured by an Arab."

That night in squad bay Roy was conversing with his Master Sergeant. Captain Rodriguez was with them. They were alone in an empty barracks beside the armory.

"I don't mind going if I won't be shooting folks. If this turns out to be a milk run, we can spend some time at the beach. That would be righteous."

"You should take a weapon, just in case."

"I'll take my old .45."

"How 'bout you, Gunny?"

"I'll take Roy's sniper rifle. What about you?"

"I got an old Thompson I like. It ain't much for distance, but it's hell in close quarters."

"Let's hope this whole thing is a false alarm. Going to the beach sounds more up my alley."

"I hope you're right, Roy. Some of the shit I've seen haunts me at night."

"Here, have another drink. This is good bourbon made in Kentucky."

"Ya know, we're lucky to have a commander like General Steele. There's nothing phony or puffed up about her. She never talks down to you. Remember those jerks before the war? They couldn't fight their way out of a wet bag."

"Johnson and Biden were both crooks. Barack Obama was a flat-out Red."

GATHERING OF EAGLES

The following morning, General Steele was standing before her assembled Marines in front of the mess hall. It was a balmy June day. The birds were chirping. There was a mild breeze coming in from the southeast off the Atlantic Ocean. No clouds were present in a pale blue sky.

"I'm asking for volunteers, unmarried volunteers. You're going to Israel to patrol Tel Aviv and to protect the IDF Command Center. Deployment will be for ninety days. It could last longer. That depends on what develops. You'll be leaving next Monday onboard C-17s from our airbase. Colonel Le Quire will be your commanding officer. Safe journey, Marines."

GRIM REALIZATION

Flying across the Atlantic.

"Whaddaya think, Gunny?"

"This ain't no damn milk run. Look at all that hardware stacked in here. We could shoot our way outta hell with this stuff."

"Right, and our asses are right in the middle of it. Say, what's that tank-looking gizmo?"

"That, my boy, is a pressurized flame thrower. It can squirt napalm about three hundred feet."

"What's that thing beside it?"

"It looks like a twin mount 40 millimeter."

"I'm glad we'll be cooking for the guys, but if things go bad we'll have to start killing again. I thought we were free from that shit. You think we made a mistake in coming?"

"No, Roy, I don't. We're Marines. This is where the General wants us."

"Gunny is right. The General sent us along to give the shave tails something to hold on to if the shit hits the fan. We know what to expect. We'll get the young ones through it."

"Well said, my man. I remember the first time I was shot at. It scared the bejesus outta me."

"I guess I'm being a pussy by not wanting to shoot folks anymore. If the shit does hit the fan I won't let you down."

"I never thought you would, ole son. But I do understand how you feel."

"Look down there. That's a battleship. I didn't think we used those anymore."

"All the signs point in one direction. We're going in Harm's Way."

They landed at the Tel Aviv Airport in late afternoon. Time changes had sent them forward a day. Trucks were waiting to load the Marines and their equipment. They were driven to their barracks then a mess hall where they were served steak and potatoes.

They were preparing to go back to their barracks when an armed escort came through the front door followed by Netanyahu. The man was eighty years old and walked with a cane, but his voice was firm and he appeared in good physical condition.

"Welcome to Israel, Devil Dogs. America is a great friend. My people are thankful you are here. The situation on the border has not materialized. My staff believes it's only a matter of time until hostilities break out. We've tried to determine the threat but all efforts have failed. We don't know what's out there or who exactly we're facing. We had planned for you to remain in Tel Aviv, but I believe your presence on the northern border with Lebanon and Syria is better served. The tanks are dug in so you will be well protected. First aid stations are a few yards behind the front lines. Multiple artillery groups can be called upon to concentrate their fire on any location. Our air force will be overhead. So will the British and Americans. Ships at sea can assist with coastal situations. Any questions you wish to ask?"

Colonel Le Quire: "Is there a password?"

"The IDF you're stationed with will fill you in. Different locations have different passwords. If you have difficulty, call our Command Center. Our Reserves are on standby."

Captain Rodriguez: "Sir, do you have any idea what we're up against?"

"Not exactly, but an educated guess is a well-equipped army with tanks and artillery."

"How much artillery do you have?"

"Israel is 290 miles in length. We have batteries of six guns stationed every fifteen miles. We're eighty-five miles across. Our ships can handle coastal fighting. Shells are stockpiled with our big guns and tanks."

Lieutenant Kozzar: "What about civilians, sir? Where do we send them?"

"The IDF knows where the shelters are. If civilians are caught in a firefight, try and find a basement. We warn everyone to get to a shelter, but some never get the word."

Roy Jones: "Thank you, sir. Thank you for a swell dinner."

3,670 MILES

"I just checked the mileage. It's 3,670 miles from here to Tel Aviv. We can't just drive in. We'll have to find a port in Lebanon and a crew to load the bomb. Then it's down the coast to the city. We'll be lucky if we aren't sunk and killed. I can't believe Master asked us to do this."

"It is strange, Yusuf, but Master probably believes a small school bus can get through. That would not be the case with an unregistered army truck."

"I know, but by Mohammad's beard, it's a four- or five-day trip through Iran, Iraq, and Syria. We'll be exhausted."

"Maybe we can get some of those pills to help us drive."

"They should have them at the military base. I will go over there in the morning."

DANGEROUS JOURNEY

"Look! He gave me a whole bottle for free. He said to break the black ones in half because they're too strong. He also gave me sleeping tablets. He said they will help us sleep after taking these black pills."

At the airport warehouse, the bomb was loaded onboard the school bus after the last three rows of seats were taken out. The 488 pounds proved no problem for the little bus. Four gold bars were secured under the front seats in case bribes arose.

"Take these machine pistols just in case. The MP40 is easy to operate. Just pull the bolt back and squeeze the trigger."

"Goodbye. Allah be with you." And they were on their way.

The first day was routine, good weather for driving and light traffic. That night they ate a box supper and slept onboard their bus with the bomb between them. The second day was more of the same thing, routine and rather boring. They ate at a diner and slept beside their deadly cargo. The third day the bomb was beginning to have an effect on them. Abdul and Yusuf were both spiritual, believing in angels and evil spirits.

"Do you feel any different?"

"I'm not exactly sure, do you?"

"I'm not ... it's like ... do you think it's watching us?"

"Oh, my ... I feel like it knows what I'm thinking."

"I don't like this ... let's stop and get out a few minutes."

They sat in the desert for half an hour, praying for Allah to protect them from the demon in the crate. Finally, they got back onboard, covered the wooden box with leaden blankets, and proceeded on their way. With the sun low in the west they began hallucinating, things running across the highway, from the constant driving.

"Let's break one of those black capsules in half. All of this driving is making me crazy. The man said it would keep us awake for our trip."

Twenty minutes later their eyes were as big as silver dollars.

"I do not like this Yusuf. I feel like I'm about to jump out of my skin."

"The pharmacist said it might make us a little nervous, but we would be wide awake and able to drive. I'm much more alert now. I feel like I can drive all night."

"I'm going to lie down a little while." Abdul took a sleeping tablet.

The amphetamine made Abdul nauseated and paranoid. He had nearly died from typhoid as a child and did not tolerate medications well. As his body fought to reject the foreign substance, he imagined the thing in the wooden crate was trying to communicate. His surroundings took on a surreal glow and he was afraid his soul was being possessed.

His slumber went on for two hours with Abdul sinking farther and farther into a deranged nightmare. The evil spirit had taken form and appeared as a monstrous black desert spider. Abdul was caught in its web and the monster was approaching. The spider began wrapping him in a silk cocoon. Abdul began screaming.

Yusuf slammed on the brakes, pulling to the shoulder of the highway. Rushing to the rear of the bus, he found Abdul half awake in a fetal position. Dragging him out the back door into the night air brought his friend back to reality.

"What is wrong with you?"

"I should never have taken that pill. I'm allergic to medications. I can't even take aspirin."

"You scared the hell out of me."

"The genie in the box had me. It was going to eat me."

"Stop that crazy talk. Come up front and sit with me."

"Did the pill not affect you?"

"I'm wide awake. I'll drive the rest of the night then we'll find a place for breakfast."

The next morning they were 370 miles from the coast. The Master called on Yusuf's cell phone to check on their progress. He was pleased to hear they were nearing Syria. The cafe offered French toast with omelets and coffee. Abdul ate a hearty meal following his escape from the horrible dream. He took the steering wheel and drove on toward Lebanon. Yusuf took a sleeping tablet to catch a few winks.

STATESBORO, SOUTH CAROLINA

Treasury had just secured a bankrupt restaurant northeast of Statesboro on the banks of the Ogeechee River. Statesboro had been hard hit during the war by Progressives stealing food, fuel, and livestock. They even took the horses and ate them. That resulted in a postwar poverty level of 43%. Parris Island is not far from Statesboro so the Marines were appointed to renovate and manage the restaurant. General Steele, with Gabrielle and Mika, flew over to meet the Mayor.

"I understand your people suffered a great loss at the hands of the enemy."

"Yes, ma'am. The communists took everything. More than a thousand of our people starved. Luckily, we have pecan trees so when the trees bore fruit that spring we survived on pecans. A few farmers had hidden their seeds for planting so we had spring onions and potatoes. When Mister Trump bombed their base, our young men from Register, Booklet, and here went over and killed the survivors. We lost nine of our boys that night. Those other towns lost fifteen."

"My men can have the kitchen open for business by next Wednesday. Spread the word in town. This is a big building so we can serve three hundred at a time. Contact those other mayors. They can bus their people over and save on fuel costs."

"What can we do to help?"

"Fresh vegetables would be nice. Is there a bakery in town?"

"We have a bakery downtown. Our farmers had good weather this year. They got more fruits and vegetables than they know what to do with."

"Do they have okra and collard greens?"

"Yes, ma'am. Collard greens and fried okra are my favorites."

"You sound like a country girl, Mika."

"Mama cooked collards and okra with turnips as a special dinner. She made her turnips sweet with sugar. She fixed everything on a wood-burning stove. I miss those innocent times."

"Have you ladies heard about our Swamp Fox? Legend has it General Francis Marion led his guerrilla fighters through these parts several times during the Revolution. Through cunning and daring, he outwitted the Red Coats and finally defeated them. His exploits in the South complemented General Washington and his army in the North. He was one of Washington's most accomplished officers."

"You must be very proud of your young men who fought and died fighting the Progressives."

"We brought their bodies home and buried them in the graveyard beside the church. There's a marble plaque in the courthouse with all their names on it. My son was one of those boys."

"I'm sorry about your son. Losing a family member is a hard thing."

"We have another problem down at the mall. Two kids on a motorbike are robbing old people. Just last week they knocked an old fella down and took his wallet. The week before that, they snatched a lady's handbag."

"Why can't you catch them?"

"It's that darned motorbike. They cut across yards and down concrete steps where a police cruiser can't go. The sheriff only has one deputy so they can't be there all the time."

"Can the city afford another deputy?"

"The city is on a tight budget and the mall is just hanging on following the war."

"I have an idea. Why don't Gabby and I dress up like old women?"

"That's crazy. You're liable to get hurt."

"Not likely. We still run our 6.2-mile course every couple of months. And we go to the gym two and three times a week."

"What about your husbands?"

"They're away in Israel. Besides, they don't need something else to worry about. Our senior citizens deserve better than two punks stealing their stuff."

General Steele assigned six Marines to dress as civilians and hang out around the mall parking lot. Meanwhile, Gabrielle and Mika performed their old lady routines, attired in granny dresses and wearing white wigs. Nothing happened the first three days.

"I'm tired of walking around in this getup like we're lost."

"You can say that again. This is boring as hell."

"Leave it up to me to get us into a situation like this."

"My wig keeps slipping down and the damn thing itches."

"Our intentions were good .... Say, do you hear that?"

"I think it's showtime, Gabby."

Two young men on a motorbike came roaring up behind them. Mika swung her pocketbook into the driver's face. She had a book inside that knocked him backward off his machine. His passenger crashed onto the asphalt with him. Gabby smashed her pocketbook over the passenger's head. The motorbike careened into a pickup truck.

The driver got up and punched Mika in the face. Mika grabbed him by his shirt, performed a backward roll with one foot planted in his midsection, and flipped him into a parked automobile. The passenger grabbed Gabby by the hair and slung her down. Up she jumped and kicked him in the groin. By now the Marines had gathered. They cheered and clapped while the lady Marines beat the daylights out of the two young men. A sergeant stepped in and bound their hands behind them with plastic ties.

"You'll be sorry for this. Our father has connections."

Mika slapped him so hard he saw stars.

"We have connections too and here comes one right now."

A patrol car pulled up and the sheriff and his deputy got out.

"Well, well, what have we here? The Simpson brats! Your daddy won't get you out of this one. You're going on a nice little vacation."

"You can't do this to us. Our father knows the governor."

"I have six witnesses that say otherwise. Two of them are standing right here. The other four are the elderly folks you clowns robbed."

"You can't do that. We have our rights."

"Put these legal scholars in the squad car, Ernie. I'm tired of listening to their song and dance."

Mika and Gabby were proud of themselves. Their fellow Marines threw a beer party for them. The youngsters were tried and sentenced to six months on the county poor farm, raising chickens and growing vegetables. Their father asked the judge to teach them a lesson. He agreed to reimburse the seniors for their losses and to pay them an additional $500 each. The father was a wealthy man. He took the seniors, the sheriff and his deputy, and the mayor out to dinner.

THE PROMISED LAND

Abdul had driven to within 70 miles of the Syrian coast. They passed through one roadblock earlier with no problem. Now they were three vehicles back waiting in line to pass through another roadblock. Something didn't seem right. The men checking cars wore no uniforms. Abdul alerted Yusuf who was asleep on the floor.

"Those are not Syrian soldiers. Something is wrong. I do not like this."

The driver just inspected drove on, and they moved up a space. Suddenly, a fight broke out. The man being beaten was pulled from behind his wheel, dragged to the side of the highway, and shot. His automobile was pulled over beside a pickup truck.

"There, on the left. Do you see that?"

"I see it. The tailgate is down. That truck is half full of things they've stolen. Those men are road pirates, not soldiers."

"Here's your P40. Open your window. When it's our turn, open the door. You get the one on the left. I'll get the ones on the right."

When their turn came, Abdul pulled up beside the man holding a rifle on his left.

"Peace be with you my brother. Would you like a pastry?"

When the thief approached his window Abdul shot him in the face. Yusuf landed on both feet and opened fire. Four men fell, clutching their chests. A fifth man ran. Yusuf shot him in the back. Two drivers behind them got out. When they saw the stolen articles, they thanked Yusuf and Abdul for their brave actions. One was a government employee transporting legal documents and a payroll. His manager had just been murdered by the bandits. They loaded his body in the backseat and everyone drove on down the highway.

"I'm going to call Master. We need help finding a boat."

Yusuf was on his cell phone several minutes, pacing up and down the aisle. Finally, he sat down on the front seat beside the driver.

"When we get within two miles of the coast there will be an open-air market on our left called 'Uncle's Place.' Take an immediate left and drive 4.5 miles to a small fishing village on the right with a sign out front, 'Boats for Rent.' We're to ask tor 'Uncle.' He owns both places. Master said he would call ahead for us. He also said to be on the lookout for bandits. I told him about the roadblock. He said success depends on us now."

Abdul drove for another hour and twenty minutes. Up ahead they saw figures standing in the highway. Uncle's Place stood out on a huge billboard. As they drew closer there was a body lying in the entrance to the open-air market. Then they saw more bodies on the side of the road.

"Yusuf, I think we're about to meet Allah."

"Keep your head. We have to get through for *Jihad*. Pull up and stop in front of them. I will get out with a box of pastries. When I have them distracted, you come out shooting. I just put a fresh magazine in your gun. May Allah be with us!"

Abdul pulled the school bus to a stop and opened the door. Yusuf stepped down with an open box. He walked toward the killers.

"Pastries, my brothers. Delicious pastries."

The leader, a tall dark man with a black beard and a jeweled dagger tucked into his purple sash, snatched the box from Yusuf then knocked him to the pavement. He took a cherry pastry and bit into it. Red juice ran down his chin.

"You think your paltry bribe will save you, dog of a whore? Oh, no, for your insult I'm going to gouge out your eyes. You will beg for death. You will ..."

It was then he noticed Abdul standing in front of the bus holding a Schmeisser submachine gun. Abdul was the last thing he saw on earth. Fifteen 9 mm rounds tore through the cardboard box, the pirate chieftain and his four accomplices waiting their turn for a pastry.

Yusuf knelt on the asphalt, thanking Allah for their deliverance.

The market was empty. Bodies lay everywhere. The pirates killed them for not being members of a strict 16th-century cult they worshiped. Yusuf called Master and told him of the massacre.

"He said to go on. We're almost there. He said Allah is depending on us."

TRANSPORTATION

"We need a Plan B in case this thing goes sideways."

"I agree. We're surrounded. Our best escape route is the Mediterranean. We got three flattops out there. Everything else is desert and bad guys."

"We need transportation, just in case. Lakota, go find us something."

When Lakota returned, he was driving a pickup truck loaded with bicycles.

"The depot gate was locked. This truck was out front so I stole their bicycles."

"Didn't they have any roller skates?"

"I guess I missed those."

"A runner came while you were out crookin' an' fraudin'. We're to stay here in the event of an attack. Three hundred more are coming to join us. They want us to plug any gaps."

"Spy satellites indicate a large force along the northern border. The Dead Sea protects the southern half of the country so it looks like a southern attack will come through Jordan. My guess is, they'll go for Jerusalem then swing north."

"Our situation looks like a double-decker shit sandwich. This is going to be a close one. It's been an honor serving with you gentlemen. Roy, I'm sorry we got you into this."

"I wouldn't have it any other way, Gunny. If you go down, I'm going with you"

They shook hands and began preparing the mess hall.

"We better get the food ready. Our guys will be here in thirty-five minutes."

"Make yourselves useful. Get the steaks out. Lakota, get that potato machine crankin'. Roy, start the ovens. We got hungry Marines coming for chow."

MEDITERRANEAN SEA

The Master had called Uncle, informing him about his two charges who were on their way. Once they arrived they gave Uncle the bad news about the murders. The man became visibly upset.

"My eldest son worked there. Where are the bodies of his killers?"

"We left them on the side of the road. Their leader is wearing a purple sash."

"I will leave them in the desert for the vultures. They deserve no proper Muslim burial. Come, I will show you the boat I have for you."

He led them to a boathouse at the end of a long pier. The craft was a 31-foot Vietnam-era patrol boat.

"What you have here is a Vietnam patrol boat. Fiberglass hull, new engines, two .50 caliber guns, ceramic shields for the cockpit, guns, and engines. She'll do 35 knots. This boat takes 650 gallons of diesel fuel with a range of 150 miles at 10 mph. She's full. Master said you have gold bars. I'll take one bar for the boat. Master told me about your bomb. My men will load it for you. We'll use the crane. Stay away from the coast. Go slow and you probably won't attract attention."

"Sir, we have four bars of gold. We want you to have three of them. We'll keep one in case we need it out there."

"The Master spoke highly of you. Come, you must eat before you go. I will pray for your safe passage."

They dined on clams and scallops. The rumble of the engines gave them renewed confidence. Soon they were miles out to sea. They were blessed with blue skies and bottlenose dolphins. The dolphins swam just ahead of the boat, which fascinated Abdul and Yusuf.

"See how graceful they are and such beautiful creatures."

"Perhaps they bring us luck, Yusuf. We will need luck."

They encountered only fishing vessels along the coast of Lebanon. The sun was low in the west when they approached the coastal waters of Israel. One patrol boat was spotted close to shore. They motored on at 15 knots. Their objective lay fifty miles ahead. The minutes crept by slowly.

With the sun touching the western sea, they slowed to 10 knots. A patrol boat farther out flashed his light at them. Yusuf flashed back. The patrol boat paid them no more attention.

"We're almost empty. I'll hold the funnel while you pour."

There were 16, 10-gallon jerry cans on the rear floor. Abdul poured until his arms grew tired. Then Yusuf took over. They discarded the empty cans overboard. A patrol boat behind them spotted the cans floating in the water. The Israeli sped up in pursuit.

"Arm the guns. I think they're on to us."

At 100 yards, the Israeli craft ordered them to stop for inspection. At 50 yards, Abdul opened fire. The Israeli boat was struck and caught fire. An alarm went out. Within minutes a second patrol boat appeared on the horizon. Tracer rounds splashed all around them. Yusuf shoved the throttles forward.

Tracers followed them in the water, striking the hull. Abdul emptied the ammunition box attached to the starboard gun, replacing it with another box of .50 caliber ammunition. Tracers flew back and forth between the speeding vessels.

"I estimate it's 20 miles. We've got just enough fuel to get there. Keep firing, my brother. Keep firing."

"They're not catching us, Yusuf. They're not falling behind either. Will it go any faster?"

"Throw everything overboard except the ammunition. Hurry! Please hurry!"

"Even the gold?"

"That too. Everything!"

Paddles, cushions, life jackets, submachineguns, empty cartridge casings, a fire extinguisher, maps, everything went into the sea.

"I think it worked. The needle is resting on 36 mph. Find something else."

Abdul found an inflatable life raft inside the bow compartment. There were rain slickers and another fire extinguisher. While throwing those overboard, a bullet sliced a gash in his forehead. Blood filled his eyes causing him to cry out. Yusuf applied a bandage from the first aid kit in the cockpit.

Now there were two patrol boats in hot pursuit. The second boat was out of gun range. On they sped toward Tel Aviv with Abdul manning the machine gun while Yusuf steered the craft from the cockpit. With ten miles to go Uncle's patrol boat was pulling away from the Israelis.

"I think we're going to make it, little brother. We've gained a half mile on them. They can't hurt us now."

Blood was pooling at Yusuf's feet.

On they sped with no clear idea of what to do once they reached Tel Aviv. Would they beach the boat and make a run for it? Or go inland seeking the Arab forces? Those options were no longer feasible because Yusuf was injured. With two and a half miles to go their engines began to backfire. At two miles both engines quit. Three patrol boats were bearing down on them.

"We're out of gas, little brother. We almost made it."

"Do you believe seventy-two virgins await us in Paradise, Yusuf?"

"The Quran tells us that is so. I believe it."

"Do you believe we'll still be friends in the afterlife?"

"We'll always be friends, little brother, always."

Abdul turned from the gun, walked over, and pulled the tarpaulin off the bomb.

"I want to release the demon. Is that alright with you, Amir?"

"Yes, my friend. We have accomplished many things together. Let us leave this unjust world together."

Abdul pulled out the titanium rod and tossed it over the side. Then he dialed the timer down to Zero. Reaching out his hand to grasp Yusuf's hand, Abdul pressed down hard on the red button.

ARMAGEDDON

Lights went out in the mess hall. The last of the Marines had gone through the service line and were seated at the tables eating their dinner. A blinding flash filled the room.

"Hit The Deck! Get Down! Get Down!"

Windows panes shattered into the room. Part of the roof was blown away. A crackling roar came from the sea. They were four miles from Ground Zero.

John and Lakota ran to the kitchen to see about Roy and Gunny. They found them flat on the deck with their arms covering their heads.

"Looks like they snuck one in on us."

"They sure as hell did. God knows how many are dead. It's going to start now and it's going to be ugly."

"Tell the men to finish eating then go get their weapons."

Colonel Le Quire walked in with two aides.

"Listen up, men. A nuclear weapon was detonated two miles offshore. They must have had trouble or they would have brought it on in. A tsunami wave washed over the eastern portion of the city. That wave was radioactive so we have a situation on our hands. Disinfection stations are being set up to save as many as possible. We've been assigned to help with the injured. Keep your weapons with you. War has broken out on the southern border. If you get any of that sea water on you go immediately to one of the decontamination centers. That stuff might kill you. There will be Israeli soldiers here shortly to help. They know where the hospitals are, cleansing stations, pharmacies, and so on. Most of our transportation isn't working due to the electromagnetic pulse from the bomb. Trucks and tanks on the other side of the country were not affected due to the low level of the explosion. You are cleared to use lethal force if necessary. Good luck, Marines."

The atmosphere in the streets was chaos mixed with fear and anger. Some were terrified another bomb would come. Others were grief-stricken over the loss of loved ones. Still, others were in a rage over what the Arabs had done. And there were the injured, thousands of them, burned, blinded, broken bones. It was a miserable and heartbreaking scene.

John and Lakota were assisting a family whose daughter was blind from looking into the searing flash of the explosion. John held her hand, leading her while Lakota tried to comfort the mother and father who, clutching one another, kept crying and asking "Why, why do so many people hate the

Jews?" Their 13-year-old son had just celebrated his bar mitzvah. Lakota was leading Samuel, holding him by the arm.

Air raid sirens were wailing their mournful cry. The walk to the hospital was depressing. Hundreds of automobiles, buses, and trucks sat abandoned. An old man with a long white beard sitting on a bus bench was raving like a mad prophet. People huddled in small groups, fearful of what lay in store for them. Homes and businesses were smashed. Hundreds of bodies and radioactive pools of water lay about. Toward the coast, black clouds rose from burning buildings. Beyond the beach, a towering mushroom cloud was rising. To the south, the rumble of war could be heard. Overhead, planes from the aircraft carriers flew to engage the enemy.

At the hospital, a group of nurses were out front on the sidewalk directing the human traffic. When Lakota approached a curvaceous blonde lady with sad eyes, she motioned for them to follow her. She led them down a hallway littered with the wreckage of war. A door was unlocked. It was a small room for the maintenance personnel. Inside was a bench for sitting, a toilet, and a washbasin with soap and towels. She spread towels on the floor for the children to lie down.

"I'm sorry I can't do more. The doctors are swamped. Lock the door after I leave."

John and Lakota had walked three blocks when they came upon a young woman passed out on the sidewalk. Her right arm had a compound fracture. They took turns carrying her back to the hospital. The same nurse directed them to a place beneath the shade of a palm tree. Off they went again, searching for more victims.

Detonation of the warhead was premature. Master had planned to get the bomb situated in one of the Tel Aviv ports then set the timer. With Yusuf mortally wounded and the boat sinking, Abdul released their monster two hours early. This threw the timetable out of sync with part of the young warriors not in position. Arab commanders began field maneuvers amid a state of confusion.

With electricity restored via the generators, Roy and Gunny were busy in the kitchen. Civilians appeared in droves. They were frightened and hungry. Ice cream set before the children stopped their crying, some even smiled. Gallons of coffee was served, ham and eggs, fried potatoes and onions, buttered biscuits. All had a calming effect on the Jewish citizens.

Seventy-seven miles west a different story was unfolding. Tens of thousands of young Muslims were attacking along a hundred-mile southern front. The sky was filled with aircraft. Helmets equipped with night vision enabled the pilots to see the men on the ground. Thus began what was later described as the 'Typhoon of Steel.' The smaller artillery pieces were firing point-blank. The big guns were lobbing 29-inch, 100-pound shells into the ranks of the Arabs.

On they came, climbing over their dead to get at the Jewish soldiers. The bloodbath did not stop them. Hand-to-hand fighting broke out with the IDF being driven back. There were just too many. With the battlefield littered with thousands of corpses, the sun came up. The fighting raged on, into the interior. Outside Jerusalem, the IDF was beginning to give way.

God proclaimed the Canaanites too evil to be redeemable so He gave Gaza, owned by the Canaanites, to the Jews. God accomplished this through Joshua, leading the Tribes of Israel. This took place in the late 13th century BC, following the Exodus when Moses led the Jews out of Egypt. The Arab-Israeli conflict has been ongoing ever since 1948 when David Ben-Gurion proclaimed Israel to be a nation. President Harry S. Truman ratified his declaration that same year.

The fighting was door-to-door, building-to-building. The Marines were brought in, John and Dakota were with them. They were manning one of the new flamethrowers. The machine weighed 76 pounds.

"I musta been crazy to volunteer for this damn contraption. It's killing my back."

"I think that nurse with the tits addled your brain."

"She was something all right, but what a terrible job. Those burn victims and the blind ones. Shooting bad guys is one thing. Putting people back together ain't my line of work."

"It is pretty awful, the blind ones an' all. They'll always be blind. Hey …. Look over yonder."

"I see it. Wave at our guys next door."

"They see it too. You're good to go."

"They said the range on this sucker is 100 yards. Hang on to my belt so it don't knock me down."

"Okay, let me know when you're ready."

"Hang on. Here goes."

"Holy Shit!"

A flaming jet of napalm shot through an open window across the street.

"That's the damnedest thing I ever saw!"

"It's the most fun I've had with my clothes on."

"Look at those mothers go."

Enemy soldiers burst out the front door with their clothing on fire. High Pockets and Mississippi opened fire with their machine gun. The men were cut down before they made ten yards. They lay silent in smoldering piles.

"This contraption is a handful. Let's go next door and see what's up."

"That flamethrower is a serious load uh whoop-ass. Let's stick together. We make a good team."

"Yeah, let's do that."

At the end of the block, a firefight was engaged. The four Marines crept along in the shadows. They found a two-story building on the left side of the street with Muslims on the second floor. Across the street, Israeli soldiers were in a second building on its second floor. War was raging seven blocks west.

"High Pockets, can you knock out that round window on the side of the building?"

A two-second burst blew the window frame off the wall.

"Brace me, John."

"I got your ass. Let 'er rip."

Liquid fire poured through the window, setting the first floor ablaze. The ceiling caught and began to burn. Upstairs was fast becoming an oven. Eleven men made it up to the roof.

"Those suckers are in a world of shit. If they jump they get shot. If they stay up there, they cook."

"I think I'd jump. I don't fancy roasting like a turkey."

"Why don't they go off the back? Oh ... that building butts against a four-story."

They began to jump. The nineteen-foot drop injured some.

"Why don't they shoot? They're not shooting!"

"Maybe they're trying to send a message."

"Send a message? What are you talking about?"

"Those young men out there were raised on a diet of hate from the time they were born. Hate Israel. Hate America. I think the Israelis are trying to show them we're the good guys."

"I don't get it. They're the enemy."

"I've been studying these people ever since we got here. I talked to some of the Jewish soldiers. Arab children are fed a line of bullshit from cradle to grave. All they know is what their crazy religious leaders tell them and what they read in that book of theirs. That's all they know."

"You're saying they're a herd of dumbasses?"

"Yes, and those ayatollahs are fanatical bastards that oughta be strung up."

"Well, if that's the case, you wanna go out there and give 'em a hand?"

"Now you're talkin'. High Pockets, keep us covered."

"Me and Mississippi are coming with you."

"Any uh you birds speak English?"

"I speak it. I speak some."

"What's your name, son?"

"My name is Malik Mohammad."

"Where ya from, Malik?"

"My home is in Egypt. I live there with my sister and my mother."

"Do you know why you're here?"

"We came to kill Jews. Jews are evil people. They stole the homeland from Palestine."

"In 1947 the United Nations established a partition for an Arab state and a Jewish state in Palestine. This was to give the Jews that survived the Holocaust a home. The Jews didn't steal anything. The UN gave it to them. You Arabs have never accepted that."

"That is not true. There was no Holocaust. The Jews made it up so they could steal the land."

"Do you believe there was a world war in the 1940s?"

"I do not know about those things. I know Jews and Christians are evil."

"Who told you that?"

"Our Iman tells us. He is a nice man who gives us sweets when he comes to teach us."

"Did you know there were civil wars in America and China in 2024?"

"We heard there were wars in foreign lands but our Iman told us that did not concern Islam."

"Are you familiar with the Great Depression of the 1930s or the Vietnam War in the 1960s?"

"I do not know of such things. But we are told the Americans are liars, just like the Jews."

Finally, John could stand it no longer.

"You wear your ignorance like a badge of honor. You don't know shit about anything. You're pathetic."

"I am your prisoner. You can insult me all you wish."

"You're not my prisoner. I don't want you. Go back to that lying Iman of yours so he can fill your head with another load of dumbass."

"You mean we are not prisoners?"

"This is your chance for a better life. Take it or go on being puppets."

"I do not understand."

"Those Jewish soldiers across the street allowed you to live as a sign of goodwill. You're free to go home. Tell your friends what happened here. Tell them the things I said. Tell them I said your Iman is a lying son of a bitch."

20 MEGATONS

Netanyahu was addressing his general staff over an Intelligence report just received.

"The wave came ashore at Reading Elementary and washed across Highway 2 for another fourteen hundred yards. The subway is flooded. The tower at the university fell. Hundreds of homes and commercial buildings are gone. It swept down the coast beyond the city limits. The north was partially spared due to all those marinas. Part of our city is radioactive. We have thousands of survivors. Our hospitals and military bases are full. Jerusalem is 40% occupied. The IDF and the Marines fought the Arabs to a standstill. Another Muslim army breached our eastern flank. Our forces there are now fighting on two fronts. Most of their air force has been destroyed and a majority of their tanks, but we suffered major losses in the exchange.

"Now the bad news. Intelligence has discovered a large enemy force hidden in the trees around Homs in Syria. Intelligence estimates this army at between 190- to 220,000. This is their reserve. Our forces are stretched to the limit now so we have two options, conventional or nuclear. Conventional is a toss-up. It may stop them. If we fail, they will reach Tel Aviv. You know what that means. I favor nuclear but that will create a backlash around the world. So many nations hate us already that its probable this would make relations much worse. So I'm asking you ..."

"Sir, you have a telephone call."

"Can't you see we're busy in here?"

"Sir, it's the President of the United States."

"Put him on speakerphone .... Hello, Mister President. How are things in Washington?"

"Washington is the usual herd of self-righteous lawyers. I'm calling about something our spy satellite picked up. There's a large army near your border with Syria. Are you aware of that?"

"We were just discussing our options for dealing with the threat, conventional or nuclear. I favor nuclear but that will create a backlash against Israel."

"It most certainly will, so don't do it. Leave that option to me."

"I'm not sure I get your meaning, Mister President."

"President Trump used atomic weapons in China which won the war for Field Marshal Feng. Trump was hailed a hero. If you employ nuclear weapons, the world will shit a brick. Let me do it for you."

"Give me a minute, sir, to discuss this with my General Staff.

Netanyahu had been facing the speaker on the wall. He turned toward the men in the room.

"You heard President DeSantis. What is your decision?"

To a man, they stood in agreement with the President.

"We accept your generous offer, Mister President. Thank you for helping Israel in her hour of need. We would do the same for you. God bless you, sir."

"I have a B-1 bomber on standby at Andrews Air Force Base. I'm told the flight will take a little less than eight hours. She'll be carrying two 20-megaton bombs. They tell me the damage from one bomb will be twenty to thirty miles."

"God help those Syrian civilians."

SEVEN MILES HIGH

The B-1 bomber was at 36,000 feet cruising at 700 mph. Temperature outside was 55 degrees below zero. The four-man crew had been in flight six hours.

"Target is 1,260 miles, Captain. ETA is one hour and forty-seven minutes."

"Keep me posted when we get within thirty minutes. Double-check your satellite readings. Got any of that fruitcake left?"

"Sure thing, Captain. Coming up."

At 350 miles the copilot began the countdown.

"ETA twenty-five minutes. Come left two degrees."

"Maintain your present course. You are dead-on target."

"ETA is sixteen minutes. Come right one degree."

"ETA eight minutes. Bomb bay doors open."

"ETA is two minutes. Target in sight."

"Bomb gone, Captain. Get us the hell outta here!"

The bomber streaked away, engaging her afterburners. Behind them, the bomb burst with the brilliance of a nova. A fireball one mile across began undulating into the upper atmosphere. The blast was felt in Tel Aviv. A hurricane of death swept among the trees.

The B-1 bomber began to circle.

"This is Lancer One reporting in. First strike looks good. Large fires are burning."

"Satellite pictures indicate the main force is three miles due east of your first strike. You are cleared to engage the second bomb."

"Course correction is spot on, Captain.

"Come right two degrees. Now back left just a skosh.

"Hold it right there, sir. ETA is one minute.

"Bomb Gone. Time to haul ass, sir!"

The second detonation at an altitude of three miles tore a wound in the forest nine miles wide. Ninety thousand men were vaporized in seconds, thousands more were burned alive. The fireballs could be seen for a hundred miles. Some questioned, were these the End Times?

The field commanders were notified about the nuclear attack. They heard the explosions. Master called warning them that another strike was underway. A second B-1 bomber had just flown out of London. A decision was quickly reached. Get out before the second bomber arrives. With 60% of their forces dead or captured, they began the long journey home.

Part II
The Gridiron

Roy was on the second floor of the Tripoli International Airport gazing through the glass. He was watching John and the last of the Marines board a military transport leaving for the States. He was staying behind because of radiation poisoning he picked up in Lebanon. Gunny and Lakota were still in the hospital with the same illness.

Roy thought back to the reason they had come to Lebanon. The Marines were backup for an IDF regiment sent to eradicate a group of Islamic rebels who survived the bombing and were causing trouble. Roy and Gunny volunteered to go with John and Lakota.

Roy jerked awake from his daydream. He had fallen asleep sitting in his chair. The guys were boarding the plane. Something about that aircraft reminded Roy of another plane ride during the Civil War. They were flying out of Eagle Pass to an airfield near Jasper, Alabama. A band of Progressives had taken over the center of town and were making sport of killing physicians.

One physician managed to escape and radioed for help. He was waiting at the airfield.

"How many, Doc?"

"They're like animals. They're killing my friends. They're …"

"Tell us how many so we know what we're dealing with."

"About nine … maybe ten."

"Are they all inside the hospital, or do they have sentries outside?"

"I saw two men out front."

"What about behind the hospital?"

"There's an alley behind the building. I don't think those hospital doors are ever locked. I can show you the way behind our bank."

"Guys, load up in those trucks. We'll take Doc with us."

The drive downtown lasted ten minutes. Doctor Flynn directed them to a street behind the main thoroughfare that led to the alleyway behind the hospital. The Marines parked behind the bank then fanned out behind the hospital building.

Two sentries out front were dispatched with silencer-equipped sniper rifles. They made their way inside though the back door. Another Progressive was sitting at the front desk reading a magazine where a dead receptionist lay on the tile floor. A 7.62mm to the back of the head ended his guard duty.

Down the hallway, they heard muffled screaming. Peering through an oval glass window in the operating room door they saw the leader with a scalpel in his hand. He was creating a Salvador Dali masterpiece from a naked doctor bound to the operating table.

The door was pushed ajar just enough to slide a rifle barrel through.

Mississippi fired. The sadist was knocked back against the wall from the impact.

"I surrender! I surrender! I'm your prisoner."

Five Progressives jumped to their feet with their hands in the air. Three dead men lay on the floor. Five terrified nurses huddled together in a front corner. The doctors had been tortured, their naked bodies revealing numerous incisions. The men standing were shot and killed.

"Doctor Flynn, tend to the man on the table. He's still alive."

"You like hurting people, don't you, scumbag?"

"I can explain ... I can't help myself ... I'm sick. I can't help the things I do ... I'm sick, I tell you. I'm not responsible. Take me to your military hospital. I'm not responsible for what happened here. They can ..."

Bad Boy shot him in the right kneecap. The scream was high-pitched like an animal with its foot snared by a steel trap. Bad Boy shot him in the left kneecap. The sadist fell to the floor screaming.

Roy opened his eyes. He had fallen asleep again from the medication. The sound he heard was the jet engines of the aircraft rolling down the runway. Roy watched as the plane lifted into a clear blue sky. A missile streaked from the far hilltop striking the port engine. With flames billowing from the stricken power plant, an outer portion of the wing broke away. The aircraft began tilting to the left.

It crashed into the trees.

"Oh, God! Oh, God!"

He ran to the far end of the tourist area and looked out. The forest was in flames where the plane had gone down. John was gone. High Pockets was gone. And those Marines whose names he never knew. He felt guilty not knowing their names. He felt guilty not being on the plane with John and High Pockets. Roy broke down and wept for his lost comrades.

HARLEM

Roy left the service and moved to Harlem to renew an old friendship. Today, he is seated at his favorite table by the window enjoying the show outside on the sidewalk. It tickled him watching the young men trying to impress the young ladies. A few made progress while others made fools of themselves. One little kid wearing a black leather jacket was out there every morning trying to look tuff. He was more adorable than tuff. A young woman tried and tried to get the attention of a hip-looking dude wearing a suit but it wasn't working. Finally, she walked up and slapped him. Roy laughed at the man's reaction. He didn't know whether to shit or go blind. But it worked. He began apologizing, thinking he had done something wrong.

A sexy young thing came up to his table, pink blouse showing too much cleavage, black skin-tight skirt showing too much thigh, purple lipstick showing too much naivety, wearing black mesh hose and fuck-me pumps. Her ensemble was topped off with a cute little red beret.

"Buy a girl a drink, sailor man?"

Roy studied the woman. She was attractive underneath the war paint and suggestive clothing. Her smile was real enough. She had good facial bones and teeth. Her eyes were clear. No sign of drugs there.

"I'll buy you a drink. Have a seat, ma'am."

She sat as requested.

"What would you like to drink?"

"Vodka and lemonade."

PART II

Roy signaled Big Jake. Jake Ulysses Grant was the owner-bartender, six feet seven, two hundred and seventy pounds. A former football great that shattered an ankle his last game. Jake was a Christian who believed in sharing his good fortune with the neighborhood he grew up in. He fed the poor and watched over the underprivileged youngsters. The local pastor sometimes held church in his tavern for the street people. Politicians came and went. So did members of the underworld. Everyone was welcome at The Gridiron.

"How did you come to be a call girl," he asked.

"I didn't sit down with you to be insulted."

"I meant no disrespect. I can see beyond your getup that you're pretty and smart. So why do you do it?"

"I'm here to give you a good time. Not answer a lot of personal questions."

"My best friend just died. I'm not interested in sex."

I'm sorry, mister. I'll move on."

"No need for that. Here comes your drink."

"You're an odd one. You don't want sex but you want to talk."

"I only talk to people that interest me. Most people are boring and ignorant. You strike me as being a reader. Big Jake is like that. He reads one or two novels a week."

"Mister Grant is a nice man. He let my mother and I stay upstairs once when we had no money for rent. That's when I got in the business. He doesn't like what I do, but we're still friends."

"I don't like what you do either, but you and I can be friends."

"Is that some scheme to get in my pants for free?"

"Not at all. You have potential. I'd like to help you find it."

"What do you know about my potential? I just met you."

"I've lived on three continents, fought in two wars, and killed more men than you have fingers and toes. That gave me insight into human nature, a person's potential, and their character. You're a good girl working in a bad business, and you know it."

"You talk like a father. I never knew mine."

"There's a vocational school a few blocks from here. You could learn a trade there. Jake and I could help you find an interesting job, something you like."

"I'll think about it. Right now I have to make some money. You be here tomorrow?"

"I'll be here. Say, what's your name?"

"Nadine ... Nadine Robinson. What's yours?"

"Roy Jones."

He watched her walk down the sidewalk. Men turned and stared. Wives and girlfriends punched them in the ribs with their elbows. Roy thought about himself as a white father to a pretty black hooker. Gunny would laugh his ass off. Gunny had died the week before in the hospital with liver cancer. Big Jake had met Gunny before he got sick. Gunny loved listening to Jake relate his inside stories about football. The dirty players got payback in the pileups when the refs weren't looking. Jake had broken a few noses in his career and knocked out several front teeth.

Nadine didn't show up the next day or the day after. Jake made a few calls and found her in the local infirmary three blocks down the street and around the corner. Roy went to pay her a visit. He found Nadine in bed, both eyes black, her lower lip split open, and her right arm resting in a sling.

"What happened to you?"

"I better not say. He'll hurt you too."

"I'm a Marine. I won't be the one getting hurt."

"I don't think I should. He has two bodyguards. They go everywhere together. You're my friend. I don't want to lose you."

"I'll be okay."

"Please don't ask"

Roy held his jacket open for Nadine to see the butt of the .45 in his leather shoulder holster. Then he held up two extra clips he carried, one in each pocket of his sport coat.

"His guards held me while he punched me. Then he twisted my arm behind my back until I promised I would work for him. He's mean, Mister Jones. He broke a girl's arm last year."

"Where does he hang out?"

"You know that pool hall beside the liquor store? He owns them both. He's usually in his pool hall."

"I know the place. What's his name?"

"They call him Desperado. I don't know his real name."

The pool hall was not what Roy expected. It was nice inside with indirect lighting, expensive lighting fixtures above six pool tables, and pictures of famous African Americans around the walls. Mohammad Ali hung behind the bar. The pool tables were occupied and several locals were seated at the bar.

"I'm looking for Mister Desperado."

The bartender nodded toward three men sitting around a table in the back of the room. Two call girls sat at the next table. A police captain was sitting with them. Roy addressed the Negro wearing a white zoot suit.

"Are you Mister Desperado?"

"Who tha fuck wants to know?"

"Nadine sends her regrets. She won't be working for a sick fuck like you."

The bodyguards stood up, big men with broad shoulders. In a flash the .45 came out, smashing the right one in the mouth then the left one in the temple. He crashed to the floor, out cold, while the other man held a handkerchief to his bleeding mouth. The police captain reached for his .38. Roy shoved his automatic between the man's eyes.

"Gimme the gun you crooked son of a bitch. Or I'll blow your fucking brains all over these pretty girls. Now get over there and sit with your friend in the clown suit. You there, take that jacket off and empty your pockets on the table and the rings and that necklace."

The terrified pimp did as he was told. Roy picked up the wallet. Eleven $100-dollar bills were inside. One of the rings held a five-carat diamond. Roy stuffed everything into his pockets.

"Place your right hand on the table, palm down or I'll shoot you where you zip your pants."

"Please, Mister."

"DO IT!"

The pimp screamed when Roy slammed the butt of the .45 down on his hand. The pool room stood mesmerized, including the bartender.

"Listen up, Flatfoot. This is off the record. You come snooping around, your chief and the neighborhood will get word you're dirty. Nadine is off limits. Any trouble there and I'll be back. Put some ice on that mouth. It will take down the swelling."

Back at The Gridiron, Roy handed Jake the diamond ring and gold necklace. Jake called a fence he knew to come over for an evaluation.

"You gota nicea stone there Mister Jake. She'll sella on Park Avenue for $50,000. I givea you 30 cents on the dollar. I makea money ana jeweler makea money. Gold I melt down ana keep. $2,000 there. That's $17,000 for you, Mister Jake. Here'sa your money. I likea doing business with you. Good day."

"We got $17,000. What do you want to do with it?

"You keep $10,000. I'll give the rest to Nadine. You mind if she stays upstairs for a while?"

"That's cool, but no hookin' outta my place."

"I'll see to it. She can stay across the hall."

MARTY

They were sitting at a table downstairs enjoying a dinner of corned beef and cabbage.

"What did you learn in school today?"

"The teacher told us about the Declaration of Independence and George Washington. It was nice learning about our country's history. I never knew any of that stuff."

"What did he tell you?"

"The revolution lasted from 1775 until 1783. George Washington and his army were almost captured on Manhattan, but they escaped across the Delaware River in a heavy fog. Fifty-six men signed the Declaration of Independence. The French Fleet blockaded Chesapeake Bay which trapped Cornwallis's army. Then they surrendered to General Washington. Washington lost most of his battles but he finally won the war. France is the country that gave us our Statue of Liberty."

"That is excellent, Nadine. Jake and I are very proud of you."

"Thank you. I'm happy just being me again, and not having to ... well, you know. I'm not a common whore anymore."

"You were never a whore, Naddie, just a misguided young lady."

"We were poor when I was little so I prayed to my Fairy Godmother to come and save us. She never came. Brother was killed in the war. Then Mama died. That's when I got in the business. Then I met you. You and Mister Grant have become my Fairy Godfathers."

"I've been called a lot of things, but never a Fairy Godfather."

They laughed. Big Jake came over and joined them. It was late, almost closing time. The place was empty except for two night owls sitting at the bar.

"We have a new boarder coming tonight. She got in Dutch with that Desperado punk and she needs a place to lay low for a while. She'll be in the room down the hall from you. She's on her way now."

"There's someone at the door. That must be her."

Shots rang out. A blonde lady stumbled in, clutching her arm, and collapsed on the floor. Roy rushed to the front door with his pistol drawn. A black sedan was pulling away from across the street. Roy emptied the .45 into the fleeing vehicle. Blood began pooling on the tavern floor. Big Jake placed a stack of bar towels beneath her head.

"They shot me in my bottom. I think my arm's broken. I'm sorry, honey. I tried to sneak out."

"Hang in there, baby. An ambulance is on the way."

Roy spoke. "Is Desperado behind this?"

"He told me he would kill me if I left ... I'm sorry I'm so much trouble."

"You're no trouble, Marty. We'll take care of you."

"I hear the ambulance."

"They're here. We're coming with you."

TWO DAYS LATER

The Captain of Police Roy had threatened in the pool hall walked in. Roy met him at the end of the bar. The Captain held up both hands in a defensive posture.

"I know you don't think much of me but I'm not here to cause trouble. I came to warn you. The pimp is crazy. He's snorted so much meth and cocaine he's psychotic. I don't take his bribes anymore. What he did to Marty was the last straw."

"Why are you telling me this?"

"What you did in the pool hall blew everybody's minds. That's the first time anybody stood up to the little bastard. It opened my eyes. He's just another asshole with money."

"Sounds like you got religion."

"It made me take a look at myself. I didn't like what I saw."

"Welcome to The Gridiron, Captain. Let me buy you a drink."

They retired to the back of the room so they could talk in private. The Captain related what he knew about Desperado and his sources of income. He made a lot of money in smuggling years ago. His pool hall was a front where men could go upstairs for a roll in the hay. Five girls lived upstairs. They were virtual prisoners. Marty had been number six until she couldn't take it anymore. The man who shot her had been wounded by Roy. He was in the same hospital as Marty. His name was Rufus Mayweather. He is Desperado's younger brother.

"Do you know his room number?"

"The room number is 217."

"I think we should pay Rufus Mayweather a visit."

"You got balls, Mister Jones. Visiting hours are over for today. I'll meet you here tomorrow morning at ten."

The infirmary entrance was a marble and glass affair with a statue of the Madonna out front.

"Looks like the Catholics have come to Harlem."

"This is a good hospital. I was treated here once. I took a bullet in a drug raid."

"Is there much of that still around?"

"I'm sorry to say there is. Too many black kids have no father. The government started that shit back in the 1960s. It's not as bad as it was but it's still bad."

"Jake and I might be able to help you with that."

The man in bed in Room 217 was a small individual, about 5'7"f and 125 pounds. The right side of his face was heavily bandaged. He had an IV in his arm and a catheter running to a bag at the end of the bed.

"You cops got no business in here. I'll tell my brother."

Roy stood beside the bed looking down on the little man with the mean eyes.

"I want you to tell your brother."

"I'll tell him all right, you crooked son of a bitch. You'll get what's coming to you."

"I want you to tell your punk-ass brother that the man who shot you came to visit. This is the gun I shot you with. If I ever see you again I'm going to shoot you between your fucking eyes. You tell Mister Desperado he has five days to close down his whorehouse. Send those five girls home with severance pay."

The eyes of hate turned to fear. He pulled the sheet up to his chin.

"Don't hurt me, mister. Please don't hurt me."

Back in Marty's room, they found her perched on a pillow looking out the window. She had an IV in her arm from a metal hospital pole on wheels.

"How's that arm today?"

"It still hurts some, but I'm mighty obliged to you, Mister Jones. You saved my life."

"Call me Roy. This is Chief Ellison. He doesn't deal with your former employer anymore."

"He's a terrible person. All he cares about is hisself and money."

"Where does he get his drugs?"

"That would be Eddie the Dude. He hangs out down by the Apollo. He sells his stuff to the entertainers and anybody else that wants to get high."

"Would you recognize him, Chief?"

"Yeah, he's a big sucker. Eddie wears a jacket with multiple pockets, and a brown derby hat."

"When you're better we have a room for you at The Gridiron."

"Thank you so much, Mister Jones. I never knew men like you and Mister Grant existed."

The next day in front of the Apollo Theater, they found Eddie. He was busy making a sale to a couple of musicians. They watched as the money changed hands.

"Hello, Eddie."

"Hold on, fellas. I ain't done nothin' wrong."

"You just sold drugs. We watched you. With your record that could get you ten years behind bars."

"Come on, now. Those were theater tickets."

"Like those theater tickets inside your jacket, maybe? You're coming with us and you're going to identify the suppliers and the major dealers in Harlem."

"I can't do that. They'll kill me."

"You have two choices. Help us clean up Harlem or you're going up the river."

REVENGE

Seven days had elapsed since Eddie the Dude was arrested. He chose to cooperate rather than spend time at Rikers Island. Two major drug busts had taken place and half a dozen drug dealers were behind bars. The drug scene in Harlem was beginning to dry up. Marty was sitting with Nadine at The Gridiron, enjoying a vodka and lemonade. They were celebrating Marty's move upstairs.

"I love it here. I feel safe for the first time since that awful pool hall."

"Mister Grant was a big football player and Mister Jones served in the Marines for 20 years. They rescued me just like they rescued you. We're the lucky ones compared to so many other girls. I think God placed us here for a reason."

"I haven't gone to church in years. Do you think it would be safe going outside?"

"I'll ask one of the men to go with us. The Chief and Mister Jones both carry guns."

Roy was coming down the stairs and joined them. He had been on his cell phone with the Chief. The news was not good.

"The Chief called. I want you two to stay indoors for the time being. The Chief thinks Desperado is up to something. A stranger has been spotted going in and out of the pool hall. The Chief never saw him before so I want you ladies here with Jake. We have a plant inside the pool hall so maybe we'll find out what's going on. He never has released those five women."

"Be careful of those bodyguards. They have guns."

"How does it feel to be away from that place and living here?"

"This place is like a dream. I keep hoping I won't wake up."

"Jake is a little bit like Moses parting the Red Sea. The Philistines aren't welcome around here."

"Do you think Desperado will ever let those girls go?"

"The Chief and I are working on that. We're waiting to hear what our young spy has to say."

That evening, Marcus Johnson, a baby-faced cop, called his Chief for a rendezvous. Roy met them in a graveyard. It was a star-studded night. An owl hooted in a nearby maple tree. Somewhere in the distance, a dog was barking.

"The crazy thing snorts dope all the time. He goes around muttering to himself. He keeps talking about 'payback.' Personally, I think he's cracking up. But he's as dangerous as a cocked pistol. That stranger you asked about, I think, is a hitman so stay on your toes. If this bastard gets the drop on any of us we're toast."

"Marcus, you've done a swell job. If you want to quit while we're ahead, don't go back."

"I'd like to give it one more shot to see if I can get a time frame on that hitter. I don't want you guys getting blown away."

"Good lad. But be careful, and get the hell outta there as soon as possible. We don't want to lose you either. That fruitcake will turn on a dime if he finds out you're a policeman."

"Don't worry, Mister Jones. I belly up to the bar with the rest of 'em."

THE GRIDIRON

"Jake, this is a coach gun, short barrel, hammers you can thumb back. They were common in the Wild West days. Keep it under the bar in case you get company. A hitman may be coming our way."

"Damn, Roy, I don't want my customers getting hurt."

"Let's hope that don't happen. I'm here and we got cops in the neighborhood."

"You think we should ..."

Gunfire down the block ... a machine gun opens up ... men were yelling ... more gunfire, closer now.

"Hit The Deck! Get Down! EVERYBODY! GET DOWN!"

A speeding black sedan goes racing by. A machine gun stuck out the back window firing nonstop. The picture window shatters, paper napkin holders, salt and pepper shakers, glasses, and plates are blown into the air. Customers are down on the floor. A little boy is crying. Roy steps over the guests to the broken window and looks out. Police cruisers are in hot pursuit of the black sedan. Big Jake comes out from behind the counter.

"Any you folks want a drink? It's on the house. I think I'll have one myself."

Down at headquarters the next day Roy and Chief Ellison were comparing notes. The driver of the sedan had been killed and the shooter was in the hospital in critical condition with four gunshot wounds.

"We hit the driver and he crashed into a building. When the shooter stepped out with that machine gun my boys let him have it. Marcus tipped us he was coming. The doctors aren't hopeful so I don't think we'll get anything there."

"Did your inside man learn anything else?"

"Yes and no. He thinks Desperado has his sights set on you and me, but he doesn't know a time or a place. I'm wearing a vest. I got one for you hangin' on the coat rack. Do you think I should get one for Jake?"

"Definitely, and I want two smaller ones for Nadine and Marty."

"I'll drop those off this afternoon."

"A raid might get some of your people killed. Why not use me as bait to lure the weasel out of his hole?"

"Yeah, and get your ass shot off."

"I could start taking walks from the restaurant. You could put sharpshooters on the roofs."

"That might work, but what if my guys don't spot him in time?"

"Good point. I could wind up looking like Fearless Fosdick after a shootout."

"What about the liquor store? He doesn't know we know he owns it. Buy a bottle."

"That's too obvious."

"How 'bout this? I set up a fake awards ceremony for me? Say on the courthouse steps. Run an ad for a few days before the event. His ego will trap his ass."

"I like it. And I'll be in the audience disguised like an old man. Have some of your men dress in civilian clothes. If this works, we'll nab the sick bastard."

PART II   135

Back at The Gridiron, Nadine was working the cash register and Marty is waiting tables. Roy takes a seat at his favorite table beside the picture window. Marty approaches to take his order.

"You shore are uh purty thang. Are ya spoken fer?"

"Yes. I belong to a man they call Mister Jones."

"Guess I better steer clear. I might get my butt whooped. I'll have a bourbon and Coke, please."

A whiskered, shabbily dressed man ambled up to the window and placed a cardboard package in the window box. Roy bolted from his seat, ran outside, grabbed the package, and ran for the dumpster on the corner. He tossed the package inside, latched the side door, turned, and ran. He'd gone about fifteen steps when the bomb exploded, blasting the dumpster lid fifty feet into the air.

Jake was rattled. "I caught up with the rummy. He said a black man in a white suit gave him $20 to deliver the box. He told him to leave it in the window box because that's our delivery place. This shit is getting out of hand. That bastard is gonna kill us all if something isn't done."

"I'll take care of it. I'm calling Ellison right now. Go back and calm your customers down. Tell Naddie and Marty to hang in there. I'm on my way to the Armory. I'll be back tomorrow.

***

2 a.m. Roy is sitting in an unmarked police van with Chief Ellison and an explosives expert, Lieutenant Atticus Clay with the U.S. Army. Atticus and Roy served in Israel together.

"The fire escape goes up to his living quarters on the second floor. There's five women up there in those other bedrooms so be careful."

"No problem. I'll do the door, a foot or two of exterior siding, and I'll bring down the fire escape. The tear gas will blow inside his room when the door goes. His ass will be hung out in the moonlight."

"You're the man, Atticus. Blow that tear gas up his damn ass. We'll be out front."

Minutes later a loud explosion rocked the neighborhood. Five women came screaming down the stairs and out the front door. Captain Ellison escorted them to the police van. No lights came on inside. The beast was trapped in his lair. They could hear him coughing from the tear gas.

"Come on out, asshole. I'll take you in alive. You'll get a fair trial."

A burst of automatic fire shattered the front window, kicking up sparks off the pavement. Roy and the Chief were crouched behind a parked car.

"Throw a few rounds his way so I can get a fix on his position."

Ellison fired two shots. Return fire struck the automobile.

"He's in front of the bar. I saw his reflection from the muzzle flashes."

Roy pulled the pin on a five-and-a-half-inch chemical grenade then hurled it through the broken window. Night became day inside the room. White phosphorus burns with a white-hot intensity when exposed to the atmosphere. The only way to make it stop it is to deprive it of oxygen.

The Captain and Roy watched the screaming man dancing about the pool room, slapping at his burning body. Desperado crashed through the front door trailing smoke, staggered to the center of the street and died there with burning bits of phosphorus lighting him up like a Christmas ornament.

Lieutenant Clay walked up. "Looks like that one's well done."

Captain Ellison was shocked from the hideous event. "That's the worst thing I ever saw. It was sickening."

"Willie Peter is a nasty weapon. An enemy can't hide when he's in the frying pan."

"Come on. Let's get the body out of the road then we'll see what's upstairs."

"I gotta get back, fellas. The men on the front gate are covering for my AWOL behind."

"You done good, Lieutenant. I'll let you know what we find."

Downstairs the phosphorus had burned out. Upstairs they found Desperado's quarters at the end of the hallway. A gaping hole was in the far wall where an exit door used to be. They flipped the lights on. A portrait of Heinrich Himmler hung on the front wall. Manikins dressed in SS uniforms stood at attention around the bedroom. A Nazi flag draped the wall behind a king-size bed. **Mein Kampf** lay on the nightstand beside a German Luger. A mountain of cocaine sat on a small antique table strewn with bottles of pills. German weapons rested against the walls. Packets of hundred-dollar bills were everywhere.

"Jesus Christ! Do you know who that is in the picture?"

"Wasn't he in charge of the concentration camps?"

"Yes, a cold-hearted, murdering son of a bitch. He took cyanide to escape being hung."

"Desperado was one sick dude. We should get photos of these rooms. The press will go crazy with this stuff."

"Keep Atticus outta this. He wasn't supposed to be here. Now, let's bag some money for the neighborhood and some for us too. You got anything that needs fixin'?"

"We need a new roof and new gutters. And I'd like to buy some dresses and new shoes for my wife. She might give me some for doin' that!"

"With all that done, your wife will wear your ass out."

"How much you think we should take?"

"From the looks of it there must be millions in here. Let's bag up $500,000 then call it in."

Back at The Gridiron, Jake and Roy were discussing the empty building next door. It was a three-story brick with an elevator. It had been for sale for eleven months with no offers. The owner had moved to Texas.

"How much they askin' for the place?"

"$200,000."

"Offer $100,000 and see what the realtor does."

"I ain't got $100,000."

"I do, tell the realtor 'cash sale.'"

The real estate agent countered the next day at $150,000. Roy and Jake countered back at $120,000. The owner in Texas said his bottom line was $130,000. So a contract was signed. A certified check was sent to Corpus Christi and Jake Ulysses Grant became the new owner.

"Where'd you get all that money?"

"Compliments of our friend, Mister Mayweather. You been bitchin' about that grill forever. Buy a new one. We can tear out the wall and expand the dining room. Maybe put in a couple of sofas and coffee tables for people waiting on a table. Get a crew in there to renovate the upstairs. You decide what you want to do with it. Don't sweat the cost. I got enough."

"Why don't you become my partner?"

"I'd rather be your friend and drink your bourbon."

"I'm serious. With a new dining room, I'll be rolling in dough. You're the ideal man. We might buy another place for old people. Give 'em a home where a slumlord isn't breathing down their neck."

"I'll scout around and see if I can't find us another bargain. Go ahead and order your grill. Bring me the bill."

"Marty is crazy about you."

"Marty is a swell lady. I'm too old to become her husband, but I love having her around. I'm 34 years older. She makes me feel young again."

"It would make her happy if you married her. Hell, who cares?"

"I don't want people talking behind her back because of me."

"The neighbors love you, Roy. So do the people that come here to eat. You and the Chief cleaned up the neighborhood. You white guys are heroes in the eyes of my black brothers and sisters. Marty would be the icing on the cake."

That night Roy Jones asked Marty Elaine Washington to marry him. She hugged him and answered, "Yes."

A NIGHT TO REMEMBER

The day Lakota Kidwell retired, his Marine buddies and several officers attended the party. General Steele was there who had moved on to a senior position with David Hanson. Roy called from Harlem. And Detective Smith dropped by for a visit.

"When you get settled in your new place, call me. I have a job you might like."

A week later Mika and Lakota had finished moving into their new home in Buckhead, Georgia. It was a brick cottage a block off Roswell Road near Interstate 285. He asked Mika if she thought he should contact Detective Smith. They knew it would involve travel and possible danger, and they had just gotten settled down. Mika said she wanted to think about it. Two days later she answered Lakota.

"Ask him what it is and ask if I can go too."

"Hello, Mister Smith."

"I'm glad you called. I'll get right to the point. There's a woman who keeps calling telling me somebody is smuggling something in at night on submarines from the Atlantic Ocean. She lives in a mansion in Oak Bluffs on Martha's Vineyard. I've been up there twice and never saw a damn thing. Some of those people are so rich they've lost touch with reality, or maybe she just wants the attention. Or maybe there is a submarine. Anyway, she's willing to foot the bill if you'll go up there and hang out a few days."

"Sounds like fun. Can my wife come along?"

"Sure, I'll see to it. I'll tell her Mika is your assistant."

The Delta flight lasted an hour. The microbus driver was brimming over with gossip about the locals, but the seven-mile ferry ride to the island was magnificent. The sun shining down on the sea gave the appearance of glittering diamonds. Dolphins frolicked playfully around the ship. It was a warm summer day. The sky was blue, the sea was calm, and there was a gentle breeze. Mika held Lakota's hand, happy to be free from the uncertainty of being a military wife.

They were greeted at the ferry landing by a uniformed gentleman driving a British Bentley. When they arrived at the address overlooking Vineyard Sound, it seemed like they had entered a Cecil B. DeMille moving picture set. A -c French Renaissance three-story white stone building greeted them with leaded glass insert windows, ten-foot oaken front doors, and massive chimney pots on either end of the structure. The grounds were beautifully manicured and the driveway was cobblestone.

"Oh, how delightful. You've arrived."

"Yes, ma'am. I'm Lakota Kidwell and this is my wife Mika."

"Come in. Come in. Mister Smith told me so much about you. I have refreshments prepared in the day room."

They found themselves looking down on the ocean through a maze of tall windows. The furniture was handcrafted and old. A rug that once resided in the palace of Louis XVI lay at their feet. Beluga caviar with minced onions, and toast points lightly seasoned with unsalted butter, sat on an oblong silver platter. Chilled chardonnay from the Chablis region was served to wash it all down.

"I understand you're a Marine, Mister Kidwell. Did you see much fighting?"

"I saw my share. I was in the Corps 24 years."

"My husband was killed in the South China Sea. He was there on behalf of the Pentagon when a bomb hit his ship. Thirty-three sailors were killed."

"I'm sorry about your husband, Mrs. Oliver. Were you married a long time?"

"Oh, no, Ollie was my second husband. My first husband died of a heart attack. He bought up distressed oil properties during the war. When the economy turned around we acquired this place."

Mika responded. "I bet you love it here. It's so elegant."

"Yes, my dear. But now that I'm getting on in years I think about my roots a lot. I was born in Kentucky. Daddy had a little stable where he rented horses to ride. I miss the simple life. Some of the people around here …. Well, you know what I mean. Would you like to see the widow's walk?"

On top of the house, they could see for miles out to sea. The upper end of the Sound, Woods Hole, and New Seabury were visible.

"Is this where you saw the submarine?"

"Yes, they come at night and they're always out a ways. The Sound is too shallow in places for submarines."

"Have you told the police?"

"Yes, they came out a couple of times at night and saw nothing so that was the last I saw of them. I thought Mister Smith might believe me so I contacted him. He was friends with Ollie."

"Tell us what you know about the submarine."

"I don't sleep much at night so I come up here when the weather is nice and snooze in my recliner. Three months ago I was awake and saw a light out at sea. The binoculars there in the box are regular and night vision. What I saw puzzled me. It was a submarine about four miles out unloading something onto a cabin cruiser. The cabin cruiser came back through the Sound but I couldn't see around the bend. I've seen that submarine twice since then."

"It could be coming on a monthly basis. When was the last time you saw the submarine and what time was it?"

"That was about a month ago. I think it was around two a.m."

"Do you mind if Mika and I sleep up here with you?"

"Heavens, no. I'll have Roger fix us some midnight snacks. Roger is the man that picked you up from the ferry. Roger lives here and looks after things and he's an excellent cook."

Mika addresses the older lady. "We can start our watch tonight. This will be like camping out."

"Yes, my dear. You'll love the stars and the ocean. It's magical with the moon over the water."

Thus began their vigil. Mrs. Oliver proved to be knowledgeable about the sea as well as the military. She had known Donald Trump through her second husband. Her first husband had told her the folklore of the region and of Spain when they were a ruling sea power. Tonight they are enjoying one of Roger's specialties.

"This is delicious. What is it?"

"I don't know. Roger surprises me all the time with his little treats."

"Mrs. Oliver, Mika and I believe you about the submarine. We enjoy your company. You're certainly not what we expected."

"You two dears are welcome to come back on your vacations or anytime you wish. I've not had such invigorating conversations since Ollie died."

"Tell us about Ollie. How did you ... Wait! Out there, I see something."

"Try the night binoculars, Mika."

"It's a submarine all right. And there's a cabin cruiser."

"What are they doing?"

"They're unloading boxes onto the cabin cruiser."

"Let me see that. Yeah, I wish I could make out the writing on those boxes."

"Can you see the name on the boat?"

"Two words, I think the first one starts with a P. The other word looks like a B or maybe a D. I can't make out the small letters."

"I think we should call Detective Smith, Mrs. Oliver."

"Right you are, Mika. I'll ring up Smitty first thing. We'll do it over breakfast."

They continued watching for another 20 minutes. The submarine sailed out of sight and the cabin cruiser disappeared around the bend of the island.

SUBMARINE

"No, sir. We all saw it. They were unloading boxes onto a cabin cruiser. Then the sub drove out to sea and the cabin cruiser came down Vineyard Sound."

"What's your read on this?"

"Well, it ain't good."

"Do you have any idea how often it shows up?"

"Mrs. Oliver thinks it comes every month."

"I got a case to clear up here. You guys go to the beach, get a tan. I'll be up in two weeks."

Six glorious days elapse. Mika and her husband are on assignment in a place that defies description. The mansion is a masterpiece, the food is Christmas at every meal, and the hostess was the next thing to a Fairy Godmother. Detective Smith calls every day. He and Lakota elect to contact General Steele in Washington.

"It sounds to me like drugs. You and Smith charter a boat and wait for the next shipment. You know the drill, no lights, go armed, and keep a safe distance. Find out where that cabin cruiser is taking those boxes. That may solve the puzzle."

Detective Smith arrived a week later. Mika and Lakota are brown as berries from the beach. Mrs. Oliver brings Roger into the discussion about renting a boat. Roger is 70 years old. He was a freedom fighter with the Pakistan underground during the rebellion. He and Lakota gaze at one another when Roger enters the room. Mika notices the change in her husband's demeanor.

"Is something wrong?"

"On the contrary, if something happens to me, you can trust that man."

"Don't talk nonsense. You're gonna live to be an old skirt chaser at the home."

"I ain't chasin' no skirts unless your pretty butt is in one."

"Seriously, what made you say that about him?"

"It's hard to explain unless you've been in combat. Men just know."

Detective Smith: "I suggest we rent a boat from the mainland. I don't want the Island to get wind of what we're doing. One of them might be in on it."

Roger Percival Finn: "I know the man who rents at the landing. What kind do you want?"

"Something with a low profile and speed."

"He has a 28-foot go-fast that can hit 50 knots. Profile is about six feet."

"That sounds perfect."

"I'll go tomorrow."

Mrs. Oliver: "Charge it to me, Roger, so nobody gets suspicious."

The days pass with everyone taking their leisure at the beach, including Mrs. Oliver. Roger rented the go-fast and docked it at the wharf below the mansion. It has been 28 days since the last sighting. Tonight, everyone is watching from the widow's walk. The night is cloudy with a ten-knot breeze creating two-foot swells. The time is 1:44 a.m.

Two o'clock arrives ... 2:15 ... 2:30 ... 2:40 ...

"Looks like another wasted evening. I suggest we turn ..."

"Look!"

A conning tower was slowly rising out of the water three miles out. Finally, the deck of the submarine appeared. Out of the mist came the cabin cruiser alongside the sub. Men appear on deck aft of the conning tower.

"Come on men. Let's go!"

Kidwell, Finn, and Smith race down the hillside to the wharf.

Roger takes charge. "Cast off. I'll take us out a hundred yards. Then we'll spread the sheets."

With black sheets spread over the boat, they lay in wait, drifting with the current. It wasn't long before the cabin cruiser passed within 200 yards. They followed a half mile behind, past Woods Hole out into Buzzards Bay. Motoring across the Bay the cabin cruiser tied up at a docking facility where a dilapidated warehouse sat in the background. In the distance, they could see illumination in the clouds from New Bedford.

"I know this place. We best go home now. We can come back tomorrow."

The next morning they found the docking facility abandoned. The warehouse doors were padlocked so they went around testing the windows. One window out back had a broken pane so Smith reached inside and unlatched the keeper.

Inside they found a Ford passenger van and dozens of boxes. There were rifles and ammunition. Then they discovered dynamite. When Smith opened one of the wooden crates he found 36 little bottles inside padded with cotton and bubble wrap.

"This bottle says Sarin. Isn't that some kind of poison?"

"Put it back in the box. It's a deadly toxin invented by Germany."

"That's odd. I wonder …. Uh-oh, the Capitol is a day's ride from here. I think I see what the van and the dynamite are for. They've got enough shit here to wipe out half of Washington."

"I suspect you're right. And it looks like they're about ready to go."

"What can we do to slow 'em down 'til we can get some help out here?"

"See if the keys are in the ignition."

"They sure are."

They took the keys and made punctures on the inside of both front tires. Then they crawled back out the window. Smith reached inside and latched the keeper. Back at the mansion, Roger prepared lobster tails with drawn butter, fresh asparagus tips, hearts of palm, and cornbread with his tangy Greek ingredients. He served them chilled sauvignon then joined the group, something he had never done before. Mrs. Oliver was delighted.

"We never went to the front lines without a good meal. That was our custom in the underground. It clears the mind and gives one courage."

"Roger was sent to me before Ollie went to China. He had a price on his head and needed sanctuary. He was a colonel in the Pakistani underground so when the rebellion failed he fled the country. His name and picture must never appear in our news media."

"I'm going to bring General Steele in on this. She has the connections to deal with foreign governments. She'll know who to trust and who not to trust. Our former vice president is a valuable asset. Victor Hanson is a patriot."

After dinner, Lakota made the call to General Steele in Washington.

"That's right, looks like they're headed your way. There are ten wooden crates in the warehouse. Thirty-six bottles to a crate, that's 360 bottles of liquid poison. The dynamite will spread the stuff all over the place."

"Keep tabs on that warehouse. There's a captain in the Coast Guard we can use. I'll send him over tomorrow."

That night they motored out into Buzzards Bay and shut down offshore from the warehouse. The lights were on and there was activity. Loud cursing was coming across the water from the warehouse.

"Listen to that. They're pissed big time."

Soon the lights were turned off and the strangers drove away.

"Call the General and tell her what we saw tonight. We have to be prepared in case they decide to move their cargo by water. Advise her to tell the captain to come armed."

The next day, a 110-foot Coast Guard cutter docked at the wharf below the mansion. The captain appeared at the front door and Roger led him into the study. Mrs. Oliver greeted her guest and introduced everyone.

"General Steele briefed me on the situation. She has men on the highway. They'll be arrested if they choose that route. I have 22 sailors onboard. I'm authorized to arrest those scoundrels if they try it by sea."

"Are you armed?"

"We have two .50 calibers forward and a 20 millimeter aft."

"We want to go with you."

"General Steele told me to humor you. She thinks a great deal of you people. You're welcome so long as you understand there may be shooting."

Two nights in a row nothing happened. As they were motoring into Buzzard's Bay on their third evening, a large craft was pulling away from the dock in front of the warehouse. The idea was to catch them in the act so they could be prosecuted. Captain Livingston pulled out into the Bay and waited.

"I'll let them get out a mile or so. That way they can't jump overboard and escape. Men, man your weapons."

With the ship well out in the Bay, Captain Livingston switched on his searchlights. A flurry of activity was seen onboard the enemy vessel as they threw open her throttle. A barrage of automatic gunfire swept the Coast Guard cutter. A sailor was struck and fell at his post. Roger was hit and stumbled backward overboard. Lakota dove in after him. Mika grabbed two life preservers and jumped in.

"OPEN FIRE!"

"Throw out a life raft. Wind it up, lads. Those bastards deserve no quarter."

Lakota reached Roger as he was slipping beneath the waves. He was unconscious from a head wound and part of an ear was missing. Mika swam up with the life preservers.

"Is he hurt bad?"

"He's bleeding but they didn't kill him. He'll make it."

"Put one of these on him. I'll put the other one on and you can hold on to both of us."

"Mika, I'm proud of you. You're a brave woman."

"It doesn't take much bravery to save the man you love."

"Where am I?"

"You're in the drink with me and my wife. Glad to have you back among the living."

"Am I hurt bad?"

"A bullet made a groove in your noggin, but you're not bleeding too badly. You'll need stitches above your right ear."

"Thank you both for saving me. One minute I was watching the fireworks. Then I wake up in Buzzards Bay. I've had enough fun for one evening. Are there any more like you back home, Mika?"

"I can think of one or two. Are you in the market?"

"I don't know. I won't leave Mrs. Oliver. But I could stand a helpmate like you."

"God, look at that."

Tracer rounds found the enemy fuel tanks and she exploded. With her transom blown out she began to settle. Captain Livingston swung his ship around and headed back for his people in the water. There would be no survivors from the deadly cargo.

Back at the mansion, Mrs. Oliver stitched the gash in Roger's scalp. She had served as a nurse during the Civil War. Roger was resting on an antique fainting couch with a glass of Napoleon brandy. She cried when they pulled him onboard the Coast Guard cutter.

"I'll have the doctor over tomorrow to give you a tetanus shot. He can take a look at that ear while he's here. We don't want our colonel getting blood poisoning."

"You're a wonder, Mrs. Oliver. I would have been dead long ago if it weren't for you and Ollie."

"Detective, you need to do your magic on that submarine. General Steele suspects it's Iranian, but she's guessing. It could be North Korean or some tin-pot in Africa."

"My staff is working on it. We should know something in a week or two. Roger, I'm sure glad Lakota got to you in time. If Mika hadn't jumped in, I was fixin' to. It all happened so fast and over she went."

Mrs. Oliver: "Yes, indeed. Mika is a credit to women everywhere. With the exception of Roger, I've never known people like you before. You're welcome to stay as long as you like."

"Mika and I appreciate the invitation. We could come back for Christmas."

"Me, too. It may be cold and snowy then, but the people in this room are something I will cherish the rest of my days. Folks like you are a rare breed."

THE HERMIT KINGDOM

"She's five miles ahead running on the surface at 18 knots. Diesel-Electric, 111 feet, 270 tons on the surface. We have no accurate records for a Sang-O II complement. I speculate 30 to 40 men. Pocket submarines are for coastal patrol and espionage. She's the poor man's version of the silent service."

"Kim Jong Un is just as balmy as he ever was. Too bad the bloke is still alive."

"Indeed, Captain. He is one warped piece of work."

"Has word come in from London?"

"Not yet, sir. They're still talking with Washington."

"Are we all set?"

"Spearfish loaded tubes one and two, Captain."

"Captain?"

"Yes, Sparks."

"Ten Downing called. They want us to determine if other ships are involved. He said the Americans want to know. What do you think it means, sir?"

"It's routine. I'll keep you posted."

The radio operator exits aft through the conning tower hatchback to the electronics room. The executive officer leans into his commander and whispers a question.

"Why did you say that, Number One?"

"Do you remember the first time you went into combat?"

"Of course, I'll never forget it."

"Were you nervous?"

"Right down to me blinkin' knickers."

"Part of the crew is green. I don't want them sweating what might be coming our way."

"Now I know why you're the Captain and I'm your Number Two."

"You're a competent seaman, Mister MacDuffy. Someday you'll have your own ship."

The pocket submarine sailed around the Cape of Good Hope and out into the Indian Ocean within sight of Madagascar. Sea swells were running at four feet. The sky was clear blue with scattered Sirius clouds. HMS Audacious maintained her five-mile vigil. A surface ship was observed in the distance.

"She's a Kang Nam oiler, 160 feet, 480 tons. She's North Korean."

"Tell Sparks."

Ten Downing Street was notified. The men in the conning tower wait and wonder. Finally, the radio operator steps back through the oval hatch.

"Close and Engage. That was the message from 10 Downing Street."

Action Stations blares out over the ship's intercom. It makes a grating sound similar to an air horn on a freight train. Interior lighting changes from white to red.

"This is your captain. This is not a drill. We are going to sink a North Korean pocket submarine and her oil tanker. Those ships are responsible for a planned poison gas attack against our friends in Washington. The attack failed. This sinking is payback and a warning for Mister Un. We have clearance from 10 Downing."

Audacious closes to 3,000 yards.

"Set your headings at zero. They're drifting. Depth five meters. Outer doors open."

"Course zero, speed maximum, depth five meters. Torpedo doors open."

"Fire One .... Fire Two."

"Estimated time 23 seconds."

The 650-pound warhead blew the engine room off the submarine. She broke in half and sank immediately. The second torpedo exploded underneath the oiler, breaking her back and setting her diesel fuel ablaze. With flames billowing 100 feet, she went down in 47 seconds. There were no survivors.

"Mac, turn us around and take us home."

"Aye, Captain. Old Blighty it is."

A Korean spy living inside the castle reported on Kim Jong's reaction to receiving the news his submarine and oil tanker had been sunk. He flew into a screaming rage, flung his cheese platter to the floor then hurled his wine bottle across the room. He continued cursing, careening around the opulent interior with its portraits and tapestries, throwing everything he got his hands on. This lasted a minute and ten seconds until he was gasping for breath. After receiving oxygen, Kim ordered another cheese platter with pickled goshawk eggs and another bottle of wine.

BUCKHEAD

"Being home, do you think you'll get bored after all that excitement?"

"Gosh, no. Getting shot at then jumping into the Bay to help you and Roger was enough to last me a week or two."

"Mrs. Oliver was awfully nice. I'm looking forward to Christmas."

"Well, this is our home now. We need to get out and meet the neighbors."

"Good idea ... Isn't that Mrs. Johnson coming up the sidewalk?"

"It sure is. I'll let her in."

"Hello, there. What happened to you?"

"Let me sit down then I'll tell you."

"Sure, come in and sit. Would you like some tea or coffee?"

"May I have something stronger? It helps my leg."

"We have whiskey and vodka."

"Whiskey on the rocks, please, three fingers."

Mika goes to the kitchen and pours two ounces of Gentleman Jack for Mrs. Johnson. She mixes vodka for herself and a whiskey for Lakota.

"Here ya go. Now, tell us what caused that bruise on your leg?"

"It's them ole boys from Midtown."

"What boys from Midtown?" Lakota was visibly angry.

"I came over soon as I saw your car. I came over to warn you."

"Who is it, Mrs. Johnson?"

"They's a gang of 'em. They took my Social Security check and stole grandmother's clock. You remember. It was on the mantel over the fireplace."

"You loved that old clock. It was an antique."

Mrs. Johnson began to cry. Mrs. Johnson was an elderly lady who lived next door and was always out walking her dog.

"Where's your doggie?"

"They killed my little Muffin."

Lakota came up off the couch. "Did you call the cops?"

"Several of us called. The police apologized. They told us it was political and they have to stay out of it."

Lakota left the room and got on his cell phone to General Steele in Washington.

"That's right, ma'am. I want to know about the politicians and their history for the Midtown Ward in Atlanta. Something crooked is going on down there."

"This sounds like something for Detective Smith. I'll call Smitty. You guys did a great job in Martha's Vineyard. I'm looking forward to meeting Mrs. Oliver and Roger."

"Ask Smith to call me as soon as he has something."

Lakota goes next door and digs a grave for Muffin. He buries the tiny dog then returns to his home. They invite Mrs. Johnson to spend the night and she accepts. Two days pass. Detective Smith calls on Lakota's cellphone.

"Atlanta has a problem, Mister Kidwell. A politician in Midtown owns a brothel there. The mayor and several members of city council have been caught on camera with their pants down. In effect, this bastard owns them. His son is the leader of that gang terrorizing North Atlanta. Big Daddy, the politician, is a gangster out of Chicago."

"That explains everything. You want in on this?"

"Normally, I would say no. But after you told me about Mrs. Johnson's little dog, count me in! What weapons do you have there?"

"One 12 gauge, and a .45 automatic."

"I got two BARs and a Thompson. I'll bring everything. Give me three days. I'll drive my armored truck."

The next day Mrs. Johnson ran over, banging on the front door.

"A neighbor called. Those boys are at the end of the street."

"Mika, you two go out into the backyard. I don't want you in the house."

Lakota got out his shotgun and pistol and sat waiting on the living room sofa.

Bam! Bam! Bam! came at his front door.

Lakota opened the door. Five tough-looking teenagers stood in the front yard. A sixth teen with muscular arms and broad shoulders stood in the doorway.

"May I help you?'

"You got money, old man?"

Lakota grabbed him by the front of his shirt, yanked him inside, slammed the door, kneed him in the groin then smashed him hard in the face. The kid tried to fight back but Lakota hit him again, this time breaking his nose. The kid hollered in pain. Lakota hit him again, splitting his upper lip and knocking his front teeth loose. He pulled the door open and shoved the punk outside. He stumbled down the front steps and crashed on the sidewalk. The front of his shirt was covered with blood.

"Any more of you gentleman need a lesson in manners?"

Not a word was spoken. They gathered up their damaged cargo and helped him to the car. From there they drove downtown to Grady Hospital.

"I want you two to spend the night in that motel overlooking the expressway in Sandy Springs. You'll be safe there. I expect company tonight. Take your valuables with you."

"Honey, let me stay with you. I can help."

"No, Mika. I could get killed worrying about you."

Lakota took a blanket next door and spread it out on the ground behind Mrs. Johnson's white picket fence. Then he brought over a pillow and his two weapons and lay down to wait. Pretty soon he fell asleep. At two in the morning, he was awakened by automatic gunfire. Somebody was firing an automatic into his house. Lakota slid the barrel of the 12 gauge over the bottom slat of the picket fence.

When the automobile began to pull away, he fired point-blank through the passenger window. Screaming came from inside the automobile. Lakota stood up and emptied the pump shotgun at the fleeing vehicle. The 00 magnum loads blew out the rear window.

He took his blanket and pillow back to his place to make sure the gas was off. The house was a wreck, bullet holes, splintered furniture, broken glass. Lakota put his weapons in the car and headed for Sandy Springs. Two blocks up the street he saw the automobile he shot at. He pulled up alongside. The man in the passenger seat was missing part of his head. The driver was slumped against the steering wheel.

Lakota climbed out and pulled the driver out on the sidewalk. He called for an ambulance, gave the location, got back in his car, and drove on to the motel. Mika and Mrs. Johnson were both in the lobby. So were a number of guests.

"We heard shooting. Are you all right?"

"I'm fine, Mrs. Johnson. Do you think it's time for a nightcap? I brought the bottles."

"Land sakes, yes! You think of everything, Mister Kidwell."

Back in their room, Lakota explained events and what they might expect for the next week or two. He took the room next door and everyone went to bed. Next morning he called Smitty.

"I beat the hell out of the kid and I killed one of his goons. That driver is in the hospital with buckshot in his puss. His beauty pageant days are over."

"Two days back in town and already you've started a war with a goombah. You need to be on a leash, son."

"They knocked her down and kicked her and killed her little dog."

"I know. I woulda done the same thing. We're gonna need backup. I'll call General Steele. Look for me around three tomorrow."

"Roger that. Don't forget those BARs."

They met in the lobby of the Comfort Inn. The four of them took a booth in the dining room next to a window. Outside a lively blue jay was hopping about on the branches of a tree beside the glass. The young jay was calling his mate. She flew in, landing right beside him. He preens her feathers for a few moments and they flew away.

"I have a martin pole in my backyard. My father had one so I put one up. They eat the gnats and mosquitoes. When I feed them they come down right in front of me."

"Mister Smith, you don't seem like the domesticated type."

"I have a cat too. She's a rescue. She's old and lazy but she seems to know when I've had a bad day. She'll climb on the couch and lie down against my leg, purring. I love the silly thing."

"And she loves you, Mister Smith. Cats know our moods. My doggie was like that. She could tell when I was having a difficult time. She would come and lie at my feet and be real quiet."

"Mrs. Johnson, Lakota punished the kid that killed your dog. Now, with the help of a few friends, we're going to put a stop to this whole rotten business. Four Secret Service agents will be here tomorrow. Lakota's old boss, General Steele, asked them to come lend a hand."

"I think it's wonderful what you're doing."

"You ladies stay here for the next few days. Smitty and I will be busy with those agents. This shouldn't take too long. Then we can go visit the animal shelter."

At 11:15 the next morning the Secret Service arrived from the airport. They met Smith and Kidwell in the Magnolia Room. Catfish and hush puppies were served.

"The General gave us the rundown on that character in Midtown. He's been indicted for murder four times but was never convicted. His great-grandfather was part of the Capone mob. He's a lowlife with no thought for anyone but himself. But he does have a weakness, that son of his. The boy is a troublemaker and the old man protects him."

"Mister Kidwell sitting beside you, put the punk in the hospital. That night they sprayed his house with a machine gun. He killed the shooter. The driver is in Grady Hospital with the boy."

"Well, by God! I heard about you Marines. It's an honor to work with you, sir. You've stirred the pot with Junior. Getting those birds to come out and play should be easier now. We just have to figure a way for Big Daddy to show his hand."

Levi, an agent from Nevada: "Kidnap the kid. Where is the brat now?"

"I like the way you think, son. He's still in the hospital. Lakota rung his bell.'"

Marvin, the senior agent: "We could do it tonight after visiting hours. Where can we stash the punk?"

"My place. It's just down the street. It's shot fulla holes but he can serve as bait. Tie him to a chair in the front window. That should drive the old man up the wall."

"It's a crazy plan but I like it. Let's hit the hospital around 10:30. They'll be in bed by then."

ABDUCTION

They left the truck in the parking area by the expressways and went in the back entrance. Marvin showed his credentials to the policeman on duty. Two Secret Service agents remained downstairs with the deputy while the other four took the elevator to the third floor. At the nurse's station Marvin showed his badge again. The two night nurses were only too happy to direct them to the smart aleck in Room 321. A guard was asleep in a chair beside the door.

Detective Smith crept up to the sleeping man and sapped him with a blackjack. Lakota caught him by his lapels and laid him on the floor. When they opened the door, Junior was watching cartoons.

"What tha ... who are you? You can't ... I'll tell my father. Stop! Help! HELP!"

Smith sapped him with his blackjack. They placed the unconscious teen in a wheelchair, taped his wrists to the armrests, and taped his mouth. The guard in the hallway was stripped and placed in the bed with the covers pulled up.

"He'll sleep awhile. Let's go."

They stopped at the nurse's station.

"When his guard wakes up you're going to have some angry visitors. Tell them you don't know anything about us or Junior here. Tell them you were tending to your patients and stick to your story. Rehearse it after we leave."

Downstairs, the two agents had maneuvered the policeman over to the front of the lobby, talking football. He never saw the men from upstairs exit the building.

"Leave him in his wheelchair. Tape his chest to the chair. Now, let's take him inside and set his ass in the window like a potted plant."

Meanwhile, frantic activity was taking place in Giuseppe's Midtown office. The gangster was having a tantrum over the disappearance of his son. One minute he was threatening murder, the next minute he was beseeching the Almighty.

"Any news from those hospital idiots?"

"No, Boss. Them nurses don't know nothin'."

"What about the jails?"

"He ain't there neither."

"I know it's that bastard on Roswell Road. Have you looked up there?"

"No, Boss. You never told us."

"Mother of God! Do I have to think for every one of you choochs? Get up there and see! NOW! GO FIND LUCA!"

Five men hurried out of the building, climbed into a black sedan, and headed for Buckhead. Lakota, Detective Smith, and the four agents were next door in Mrs. Johnson's front yard behind her picket fence.

"You think they'll show tonight?"

"Right now, Mister Big is pacing the floor with a bee up his butt. His men will show."

"Looks like Junior's awake. He's rocking back and forth in his wheelchair."

"If he turns it over, I'll go set 'im back up. He needs to be in plain sight."

"Well, there he goes."

"Come on. Cover me."

The two agents head for the front door just as a black sedan pulls up to the curb. Gunfire erupts. Bullets strike the front of the building. Once inside, they set Junior back up for all to see. The gunfire stops.

"Are you hurt?"

"He got me in the ass. It hurts like getting stung by a damn wasp."

"Drop your pants and let me see."

"Damn! You got another asshole."

"Don't fuck around. What's it look like?"

"They shot a piece out of your left butt cheek. It ain't too bad. I'll get a hand towel out of the kitchen. You can put that in your shorts to help stop the bleeding."

"You in the house. Bring Luca out and we'll let ya go."

"Let's see if we can lure 'em out into the open. They don't know what's next door."

"Fuck you, spaghetti snapper. Come and get the worthless prick."

A machine gun blast blew off the lower section of the front door.

"Hey, wop boy, your hoochie mama does the deed for five euros."

Another blast blew out the glass panes in the top and bottom sashes left of the picture window. The two agents began laughing. Luca was terrified he might get shot.

"Hey, scemo, wanna hear your mama's favorite tune? It's called 'Don't You Just Know It.' This is her mating call .... Gooba Gooba Gooba Gooba ... Ah-Ha Ha Ha ... Ah-Ha Ha Ha ..."

Gunfire blew out the two right window sashes into a thousand pieces.

"Dayyyoo ... Gooba Gooba Gooba Gooba ... Gooba Gooba Gooba ... Ah-Ha Ha Ha ... Ah-Ha Ha Ha"

"You Stop That! My mother teaches eighth grade."

"Ah-Ha Ha Ha ...Ah-Ha Ha Ha ... Gooba Gooba Gooba Gooba ... Dayyyoo."

"Stop it, I say. You stop that right now!"

"Gooba Gooba Gooba Gooba ... Ah-Ha Ha Ha."

PART II

The shooter came out from behind the black automobile, shaking his fist and cursing. McCoy leveled his carbine on the windowsill and fires.

"Son of a bitch! You got 'im. We oughta revive Huey Smith and the Clowns. Go on tour. Make a million bucks."

"I'd be happy just to get some pain medicine. My ass hurts like a mother fucker."

More gunfire from the automobile. A barrage opened up from the picket fence. A man standing beside an open car door was struck. The driver took off. Another man lay in the middle of the street.

"Come on out, guys. The party's over."

"McCoy needs an ambulance. Looks like Mister Badass in the street could use one too."

"Where'd you learn to sing like that?"

"We heard that song on TV. It was so funny we practiced singing it."

"You hurt bad?"

"Not bad, but I sure could use a shot."

"Ambulance is on the way. Let's check on that dude in the street."

"Two of 'em got away. The driver may be hit."

"Lakota, your house looks like forty rows uh bad corn."

"We'll stay with Mrs. Johnson while it gets fixed."

"Here comes the ambulance. You go on, McCoy. Hank, you go with him. Keep your weapons. The man in the street is dead. We'll catch up after we get rid of these bodies."

MIDTOWN

Giuseppe knew he was in trouble. Four of his men were dead and two were in the hospital. Luca would have to wait until he figured things out. Who are these people? Who sent them? How many are they?

"Tell me again what happened."

"We drove up to da house an' dese two guys run inside. Dey sat Luka up in da front window in-a wheelchair. Luca was tied in dis wheelchair. We shot da place up some den told 'em we'd let 'em go if they'd give us Luca. Den dey started singin' dis crazy song. It got under Rocco's skin so dey started insultin' his mother. Rocco come out from behind da car and dose guys in da house shot 'im."

"They was singin' at ya? That's crazy. Was Luca all right?"

"Yeah, Boss. Luca looked okay."

"Well, get on with it. What else?"

"When Rocco got shot we started ta rush da house. Den we got ambushed. Dey was men behind dis fence next door. When Joey got shot I ran for da car. Me an' Aurelio got away but he was shot too. He drove to da hospital an' I got a cab here. Da gas tank was leakin' all over da parking lot."

"Here's what we're gonna do. You three go back to Buckhead. One uh yas stays there. One goes to Sandy Springs, and the other one goes up ta Roswell. Check out the motels. Look for cars with official license plates. They'll be holed up in one uh them motels."

SANDY SPRINGS NEWS

"I been thinkin', Smitty."

"Well, don't hurt yourself."

"How much longer can we keep dealing with dirtbags before one us gets killed?"

"Good question."

"I put in over 20 years in the Marines. Several times me and the fellas got lucky. Lately, I've been involved in three more scrapes. You were in the last one when Roger got hurt. Odds are, one of these days, our number is coming up."

"Here's how I look at it. Part of the stuff we do is dangerous, but I like to think we're helping people. Like that business with the submarine. We probably saved a thousand lives, maybe a lot more. If we'd gotten whacked doing our job, we would have died for an honorable reason. Same thing when John killed that government rat, you guys did the country a favor."

"I never thought about it like that. Maybe I'm thinking too much. I want Mika to have a safe and comfortable life. But I keep going away on these missions."

"I was schooled in reading faces and people's emotions when I became a detective. I saw something in Mika you may have missed. She relished being onboard that Coast Guard ship. The unknown danger fascinated her. Then, when you dove in after Roger, she went over the side before I got my shoes off. Mika is cut from the same bolt of cloth as you, my friend. Your wife has the face of an angel, but down deep inside she's a lot like you and me."

"I'm glad you told me. I didn't know that."

"We need to get organized on this creep downtown. By now he knows we're after him. We know his weakness is his son. So how can we exploit that?"

"Get the police involved?"

"I was thinkin' along those lines. The police department up here is different from the one downtown. The editor of the local paper is a straight shooter. He could run a piece on his front page about the kid being arrested and held in the local lockup. 'Son of Chicago Gangster Arrested' and so on. All we'd have to do is wait for Big Daddy to come to us."

Two days go by. A special edition of the **Sandy Springs News** is printed. A mugshot of Luca is featured on the front page. His nefarious exploits in North Atlanta are mentioned. A photo of the Atlanta mayor was next to his. A question was asked, "Why was this criminal activity allowed to go on for six months?" His father's photo was down below with the caption, "Chicago Gangster Rules Atlanta Underworld." The newspaper sold out in half a day.

Detective Smith met with the Secret Service agents upstairs in the motel. Lakota was lodged on the first floor with Mika and Mrs. Johnson. Two Browning automatic rifles were laid out on one of the twin beds. Lakota was teaching Mika how to operate the BAR.

"To release an empty magazine just push the button on the trigger guard. A new magazine goes in, bullets forward, then tap the magazine with the heel of your hand. When it clicks, it's seated. To charge the weapon, pull the bolt all the way back then let go. That will drive a round into the chamber. It kicks a little so hold the weapon tight and point it at your target."

Mrs. Johnson: "Do you really think they'll try coming here?"

"Detective Smith thinks Giuseppe is some kind of psycho. Smitty studied his records. He says he's mentally unstable, dangerous, and very aggressive. That's why the boy got away with so much. The man exhibits the traits of a narcissist. He doesn't care about anyone but himself and his son."

"My goodness, he sounds scary."

"There are two cops outside and two agents in the lobby. We're safe."

GUNFIRE!

"Come on, Mika. We better check the lobby."

Running down the hallway with their weapons, they stop at the corner. Two men in the doorway are firing automatic weapons. Marvin and Smitty are lying on the lobby floor. Levi is behind the front desk with only his handgun. Another blast and Levi falls to the floor.

Lakota steps out and fires a long burst. The two men go down. A third man behind them opens fire. Lakota is hit.

"Come on." They ran for the dining room. Lakota is hit a second time. His rifle clatters to the floor.

Mika takes him by the arm, half-pulling, half-dragging her husband across the open space. The dining room is empty. She pulls a sofa out sideways and places Lakota behind it. Mika dumps a long metal table of salads and dressings on the floor. This, she turns up on its side on the sofa cushions. Another metal table, she slides in against the front of the sofa.

"Hang on, baby. I'll take care of you."

"Here's an extra magazine ... do you ... remember ... how to reload?"

"Push the button. Seat the magazine until it clicks. Pull the bolt all the way back and let go."

"My arm is broken ... I have no feeling ... in my hand ... I love you, Mika ... If I'm going to die ... I love you ..."

"I won't let that happen. You want a baby, remember? I'll have our baby."

Lakota passes out.

The shooter strolls into the room. He is unaware Mika has a weapon. Giuseppe appears in the doorway holding a submachine gun. Mika fires her BAR. The shooter sprawls dead. She empties the remainder of her magazine. Pieces of wood, drywall, and shards of glass fly about the doorway. The gangster is struck in the hip.

He hobbles out onto the floor using his weapon for support.

"You're done for, bitch. You got no bullets left. I heard the click. I'm gonna kill you and that loser husband of yours. Ya hear me? I'm gonna kill you. You're gonna die, you miserable cunt."

He fires a long burst that bangs into the metal table on the sofa. He fires another burst. Plastic flowers rain down from a window arrangement above their heads. He's 40 feet and closing.

The psycho continues hobbling across the room, raving like a maniac, leaving a trail of blood behind. Mika is terrified. Her life flashes before her eyes. Her love for Lakota drags her back to reality. If she fails, Lakota will die.

Mika has only seconds. She presses the button on the trigger guard. It doesn't release. She tries again.

"Please, Great Spirit. Please help me."

She jabs it hard with her thumb. It pops out. She seats the fresh magazine and pulls back the bolt. Giuseppe peers over the top of her barricade. He raises his submachine gun, pointing it down at her.

Mika pulls the trigger. The automatic roars to life.

The 30-06 rounds exiting the top of Giuseppe's head take part of his brain with them. The mobster crashes backwards on the floor. Mika gathers her unconscious husband in her arms and prays.

Their trip to the hospital was a nightmare. Lakota's heart stopped beating so the paramedics used the paddles. Two hours into surgery a priest was summoned. Mika couldn't stop crying so one of the physicians gave her a sedative.

Mika opened her eyes. She was in bed wearing a hospital gown. General Steele was sitting beside the bed. Roy Jones was in the room and Mrs. Johnson. A bouquet of daisies, her favorite flower from childhood, sat in an attractive urn on the dresser. It was dark outside.

"He's dead, isn't he?"

The General reached for her hand.

"No, Mika, but he's badly hurt. Two specialists worked half the night putting him back together. They were losing him so a priest came and prayed. God answered his prayer."

"But it's still dark."

"You went into shock so the doctors kept you asleep for 24 hours. The shooting was two days ago. Witnesses told us what you did. You're an amazing woman, Mika Kidwell."

"Thank you, Roy. Thank you all for being here. How bad is he?"

"They managed to save his right arm. He lost a kidney and a section of intestine. He'll be in intensive care for several days. Prognosis looks good."

"When can I see him?"

"Another day or two. He's still doped up."

"I have to pee."

HOME SWEET HOME

Lakota and Detective Smith were sitting in Mrs. Johnson's living room watching an old TV series, **Reacher**, with Mrs. Johnson's new puppy, a wiener dog. The little dog was sitting on the sofa between the two men. Mika and Mrs. Johnson are out in the kitchen preparing lunch.

"Did you get hold of Levi?"

"Yes, he's off his crutches and doing well in therapy. He said to tell you 'hello.'"

"It's a shame about Marvin. He was a good agent."

"I was right about your wife. If it hadn't been for her we'd all be dead. Giuseppe was a psycho and that son of his is just plain mean. He deserved what he got, prison or the Army."

"Ya know, if he can make a go of it in the service he could turn out okay."

"And if he screws up, it will be blanket parties and the brig."

"I hope he makes it. His father made him what he is. He could change."

"Time for lunch, boys. Come to the table."

NEW YORK CITY

Roy went home to his wife after visiting Lakota in Intensive Care. Their meeting made a lasting impression on Roy. Lakota had always been proud and strong. The man he found lying in bed reminded him of how fragile human beings really are. When he was about to leave, Lakota said something profound.

"Don't waste another minute of your life. Love the ones who love you. The hourglass is running."

Back in Harlem, Roy was greeted by Big Jake and The Gridiron staff. Nadine hugged his neck and Marty kissed him. Roy told them about Mika's heroism. Everyone was fascinated over her gunfight and Lakota's brush with death. They were grateful Detective Smith survived.

Roy thought about Lakota's warning about the hourglass. Gunny and John were gone. Lakota was recovering from his ordeal. That left The Gridiron crew and his wife. They were his family and he loved them.

Jake was happy to have Roy back. Renovations on their three-story brick building next door had just been completed. It was Sunday and the restaurant was closed.

"We got eighteen apartments up and five offices on the first floor. The elevator is fixed and a new HVAC unit is on the roof. I got a beauty salon and a barber shop ready to move in."

"That's swell, Jake. You think we should furnish the apartments?"

"I checked with Goodwill. They'll do it for $1,000 apiece."

"That's very reasonable. Go ahead. I'm going in to check with the Captain. One of his men wants an apartment."

Down at the station, Roy is ushered into the Captain's new office. It has a window with a view. On the wall, he has a photograph of Roy and himself in Desperado's bedroom with the mannequins wearing SS uniforms.

"You've gone up in the world."

"Yeah, I love my new office."

"Why do you keep that awful picture?"

"It reminds me of my grandfather. He served with the Navy at Guadalcanal and Okinawa. He never talked about it much. But once he told me about the Kamikazes at Okinawa. He said hundreds were shot down but 10% got through. He told me 5,000 sailors were killed by those planes."

"I read about that at Parris Island. I read about the European Theater too. Hitler might have won if he'd let his generals run the war. The Germans were stupid at Dunkirk and the Battle of Britain. Hitler made terrible mistakes on the Eastern Front."

"The Japs did the same thing at Pearl Harbor. They left the fuel tanks and the dry dock intact."

"Our Civil War was no picnic. I'll never forget how close we came in Lenoir City guarding that Tennessee dam. We lost 77 men. I just visited with a buddy of mine in Atlanta that got shot up pretty bad. He reminded me to make the most of things while we're still here. He said, 'the hourglass is running.'"

"Remember me telling you my wife might give me some over a new roof and some new dresses? Well, I did it. And she's been a tiger in the bedroom ever since. Used to, it was once, maybe twice, a month. Now it's every other night. Buy your wife a pair of new shoes and see what happens."

"I'm almost afraid to after that confession."

They both laughed. Roy told him the apartments would be ready as soon as the furniture was delivered.

"You remember our spy, Marcus Johnson? He's living in a dump over off 119th Street. He accused his landlord of price gouging so they kicked him out. He's got 'til the end of the month."

"We'll be ready. I'll put him on the second floor overlooking the street. It has a balcony."

"How much is it?"

"Six fifty a month."

"Damn! That's cheap. He's paying $850 now for a postage stamp with rats."

"You oughta turn that bastard in."

"I already have. The Health Inspector will be paying the landlord a visit in a couple of days. He's going to tear him a new one over all the health violations."

"Any bad shit goin' on lately?"

"A rash of burglaries. One auto theft and one mugging. Oh, and some punk hanging out around the grammar school is stealing lunch money. You mind looking into that?"

"What's he look like?"

"Skinny kid, fourteen or fifteen, wears a hoodie and white sneakers. I ain't had time to deal with it with all these burglaries. You'd be doing me a favor."

"I'll check into it tomorrow morning."

Roy arrived at the grammar school at 7:15. To his surprise, the kid was standing on the sidewalk leading up to the front door. Roy watched as the young man pulled a youngster aside and held out his hand. The boy placed a dollar bill in the outstretched palm, turned, and went inside. The same thing happened with a young girl. Roy approached the youth.

"Son, you're outta line. Stealing from children will land you in prison one of these days."

"You ain't no cop. You can't arrest me."

Roy pulled out a pair of handcuffs and dangled them in front of the boy. Then he opened his jacket revealing the .45 automatic in his shoulder holster.

"If you run, I'm authorized to use this. A .45 slug makes a nasty hole."

"I won't run, mister. Please don't shoot me."

"What in the world are you doing out here stealing from these kids?"

"I'm the Artful Dodger."

"You're a what?"

"It's like the movie **Oliver**. There's five of us Artful Dodgers. Mister Buckingham is our Mister Fagin. It's all a game. We bring him money and things he can sell, and he feeds us and gives us a place to sleep."

Roy recalls the Chief's comments about a rash of robberies.

"Are you hungry, son?"

"I had half an apple for breakfast."

"Would you like some ham and eggs and a glass of cold milk?"

Back at The Gridiron the boy stuffs himself on Jake's cooking. The Chief was summoned and he meets with Roy and the young man. Turns out he's an orphan who ran away from the orphanage after he was caught stealing from the money jar in the kitchen. He cries because he believes he's going to prison.

The boy looks at Captain Ellison with tears in his eyes. "You gonna send me away?"

Roy pats the boy on the shoulder.

"I can change your life if you want to change. You can work around here bussing tables, hauling out the garbage, keeping the place clean, and going to school. You will answer to the big man behind the counter. There would be a room for you upstairs."

"Why are you doing this?"

"A friend of mine in Atlanta told me a few nights ago, 'the hourglass is running.' You have a future before you. It can be positive or you can end up in jail or dead. Do you want the job?"

"Oh, golly, Mister Jones. I want the job. I surely do."

FAREWELL, MY LOVE

Mister Buckingham's hideaway consisted of a ramshackle building on pilings on the riverbank of the Harlem River. Abandoned years earlier, Buckingham has jerry-rigged electricity from a power pole on Harlem River Drive. The door was unlocked.

"Mister Fagin, I presume."

"What ... who are you ... what do you want?"

"Charles told us you have jewelry for sale."

"Oh, yeah, that ... I have a drawer full."

Buckingham pulls out a wooden drawer from a dilapidated dresser. The drawer is filled with rings, watches, necklaces, and a .38 caliber revolver. Buckingham palms the revolver. He throws the drawer at Ellison, brings his gun up, and fires. Roy fires. The .45 spins the man around and he crashes through a table and chairs.

"He got me. I didn't think he was armed," Ellison said.

"Come on," Roy said. "I'm taking you to North General on 122nd."

Captain Ellison was rushed into surgery. Roy calls his wife. She arrives fifteen minutes later. Roy is struck by how attractive she is to be middle-aged.

"Get a grip, Ann. He's been shot but he's going to be okay."

"You're telling me the truth, aren't you? Luther isn't going to die, is he?"

"I swear to you, Ann. The doctors are taking the bullet out right now."

A physician approaches.

"He has some internal damage, but we're taking care of that. Detective Ellison is going to be as good as new."

Ann sits down and cries. Roy places his arm around her.

"Luther told me you have a new roof and gutters. I bet that's something."

"He told me about you. He ... He told me ... about that awful man with the pool hall. He calls you his brother. I'm thankful you two are friends. I want him to retire. He's too good to be chasing after thieves and murderers."

"Do you think he would be happy retired?"

"Probably not. I'm just being selfish. He loves his police work."

"Did he tell you how he helped clean up my neighborhood?"

"Yes, he did. He said you're part owner of a restaurant over there."

"Mister Grant is my partner. We have some apartments. I would like you to come and stay with us until Luther gets out of here. The restaurant is right next door."

"This is the second time he's been shot. I worry about him all the time."

"You would like Big Jake and Nadine and my wife, Marty. Come stay with us, Ann."

"I think I will. I don't want to be by myself right now."

Back at The Gridiron Mrs. Ellison was introduced to everyone, including young Charles who just wiped off her table.

"That young man. He's so cheerful."

"That's one of my rescues. Luther and I took him out of a crime scene. Charlie works here now and goes to school. He's a good boy."

"You must be very happy here with all these wonderful people. Your wife is lovely. I think I would like a cheeseburger. I haven't had a cheeseburger in ages, and a Coca-Cola, please, sir."

"I'll tell Jake."

Thud! Pedestrians begin yelling. A woman is screaming abuse. Nadine hurries to the front door and looks out.

"Oh, My God!"

Roy runs out onto the sidewalk. Jake is by his side. So is young Charles.

The blue skirt and white blouse and the tiny jeweled purse lying on the pavement Roy gave her for her birthday. Mail is scattered all over the street. The small body is twisted at an odd angle by the drunk driver that ran over her. Her shoes were knocked off. A crowd gathers. Roy kneels by Marty's side, weeping brokenly. Charles is crying. So is Jake and Nadine.

Marty's funeral was held at Covent Avenue Baptist Church. Roy sat between Ann and Nadine in the front pew. Detective Ellison, Charlie, and Jake sat with him. The Gridiron staff was seated in the second pew. Two hundred people from the neighborhood gathered to pay their respects.

"Lord, a cherished soul entered your Kingdom four days ago. Martha Jones was a wife and beloved member of Harlem. Grant unto her eternal peace and shine down your perpetual light of healing upon those who loved Marty. Show us the way, Lord, that we may place this tragedy behind us, and dwell in the sunshine of your grace."

Her eulogy went on for another 30 minutes. Afterward, everyone retired to the dining hall for coffee and cake while the casket was being placed at the grave site. Detective Ellison was using a walker to stand beside Roy as his wife was lowered into the ground. Then it was over. Jake drove Roy and his friends back to The Gridiron.

"Would you like me to fix you a drink?"

"Yes, that would be nice."

"Fix me one too, Jake."

Roy was taking his second sip when five women from the neighborhood filed through the front door carrying an assortment of cooking utensils. They set their wares down on the counter and turned to address the gathering.

"Our Food Club chose us to bring over our specialties to help address this sad occasion. We're mighty sorry Marty is gone. My name is Missy Brown. I brought you a skillet of Cornbread Harriet Tubman style. This will tickle your taste buds, Mister Roy. Try it with salted butter."

"God bless you, Mister Roy. My name is Rebecca Jordan. What I have is a collard greens recipe handed down from my people who were slaves. Herbs and green onions go in it, but the main ingredient is a big ole ham bone. Use a tablespoon of vinegar when serving."

"They call me Fanny, but my real name is Elizabeth Brice. None uh you white folks ever had 'coon before, but I got him legal at the butcher shop.

Slow-baked with cornbread stuffing an' marinated with bacon grease and brown sugar. 'Coons make good eatin'. 'Coons an' possum was all we had back in the old days."

Big Jake could keep quiet no longer. "Hold on a minute. I got to sample these vittles …. **ummm** …. **ummm ummm** …. This food is delicious. What else y'all got?"

"That sure was a sweet compliment. I'm Loraine Green. I been livin' here in the neighborhood 50 years and then some. Mister Jones and Mister Ellison sho is welcome newcomers. We love y'all. My specialty is turnips and roast pork with carrots and onions. Turnips give it a sweet taste."

"I reckon that leaves me to bring up the tail end. My name is Jonnie Washington. I love baking pies. Lemon is my favorite pie. This recipe is not old. It's right out of our Food Club Cookbook."

"Ladies, would you and your Food Club be interested in selling your creations through my restaurant? There's room in here to grow. We could operate on a 50 - 50 basis. You'll make a lot of money."

Roy was coming out of his melancholy. "And after you get a nest egg saved up, I'll find you a reasonable place to buy and set up your own restaurant. We could pull it off in maybe six months."

"Land sakes, I never dreamed such a thing. I like your proposal, but we'll have to take it for a vote before our membership."

The vote was taken and all 25 members were enthusiastic over the prospect of owning a restaurant. Roy visited the Food Club every week to get a handle on the size kitchen they were going to need. With four or five cooks in a kitchen at one time, it had to be large enough. He found a foreclosure in the courthouse records that the city had taken over for back taxes. The owners were deceased and it had been for sale twice. But it was perfect for what Roy and Big Jake had in mind. The kitchen was expanded to 30 feet with all new appliances purchased from an appliance store going out of business. When the Food Club was shown the property, several of the ladies cried. They were so happy that Roy and Big Jake had taken an interest in them.

Three weeks later Mama's Place opened to a full house. It wasn't long before **The New York Times** took an interest in Mama's Place. After that, the ladies never looked back. An old abandoned building in Harlem soon blossomed into a four-star restaurant.

NEW BEGINNING

His cell phone rang at 9 a.m. Mika was on the other end. Lakota had passed away in his sleep. Her best friend was dead. Lakota would find his white stallion waiting for him in that faraway land of the Great Spirit where he would make camp and wait for her. She cried a little, but for the most part, she was very brave. Roy told Mika he would fly down the next day.

Services were held at Mount Paran Church near Sandy Springs. General Steele came. So did Detective Smith. Lakota was 72. He had never fully recovered from his gunshot wounds. Nevertheless, he led an active life in the community.

Mrs. Johnson died. He and Mika missed the sweet old lady. The world was changing. Too many lawyers, and too many politicians. Lakota felt his life was ebbing away, so he withdrew from society to spend more time with his wife. They were inseparable those last two years.

General Steele made arrangements with Arlington National Cemetery. They flew up together for the ceremony. Following Taps and the folding of the flag, they drove into Georgetown for dinner.

"Have you thought about what you're going to do now?"

"Not much .... Teach, maybe."

"I have some lady friends in Harlem who just opened a restaurant. They could use some help."

"Doing what?"

"Ordering supplies, paying bills, dealing with customers."

"I don't think I'd be any good at kissing somebody's behind."

"This is Harlem. You put the difficult ones in their place."

"Where would I live?"

"I live on the second floor over The Gridiron. There's a spare room across the hall from me. If you stay, we have apartments next door."

"I don't know. It sounds like a lot of work."

"It is a lot of work, but you'd be doing good deeds and helping yourself at the same time."

Mika studied on it a spell and decided to give it a try. Mrs. Ellison met her at the Ronald Reagan Airport.

HELEN

Her second week at Mama's Place, she was filling in for a sick waitress.

"May I take your order, sir?"

"I've been sitting here two whole minutes, and you just show up?"

"I'm sorry, sir. We're shorthanded today."

"Don't give me any of your sass, woman. I'm with the mayor's office. I'm not accustomed to waiting. You don't know who you're dealing with. I could …"

Mika slapped his face so hard his false teeth flew out onto the table.

"How dare you! I'll pull the license on this place. I'll sue you. I'll … I'll …"

Two truck drivers sitting at the table next to the mayor's assistant were looking at him like a hungry mongoose eyeing a tasty snake. He quickly realized he was in over his head.

"May I take your order now, sir?"

"Yes, ma'am. I'll have the country ham, mashed potatoes and gravy, collard greens, and sweet tea, please."

Word went out around East Harlem. "Don't mess with the Indian."

To her surprise, Mika took a shine to the African American ladies. They were a close-knit group, laughing and joking while creating their special dishes. One older woman in particular she found herself drawn to. Helen was 84, grew up poor in Arkansas, became a dancer at Radio City Music Hall, and served three years in Sing Sing Prison.

"Lord, honey, I was a rounder back in the day. Dancing was great fun. Men threw themselves at your feet, literally. Well, this one fellow got me hooked on cocaine. I musta put a hundred pounds up my nose. Anyway, he was Mafia and had connections in government and all over the place. He was a sweet-talker so I wound up marrying the fool. He was into drugs, prostitution, bootlegging, and God knows what else. It didn't make no never mind so long as the champagne and cocaine kept comin'.

"Know what I liked best about that man? He had a joystick ten inches long. That sucker could ring my chimes like the bells of Saint Mary's."

"Oh, that's awful."

"Don't I know it!" They both cackled.

"Anyway, I got to helping him with his drug business. That's when it all went sideways. He was in a shootout one night with the Feds and got his ass killed. The whole gang got arrested then they come after me. I kept my mouth shut so I got three years in prison.

"Anyways, I slicked 'em before they arrested me. I shipped a trunk full of money to Switzerland. One of the accountants told me how to do it so it couldn't be traced. So I got me a Swiss bank account under the name 'Pearly.' That's what they called me when I was a dancer.

"All my people are dead now and I ain't got no children. The doctors give me maybe six months to live so that's why I'm giving you my account number and password. You're a kindhearted soul, Mika. Put the money to good use here in Harlem."

"I'm going to miss you, Helen. You're my dear friend. Roy and Jake will know what to do. I'll get them involved. How much is in the account?"

"About $12,000,000."

Helen passed away four months later. Mika withdrew $16,000 and gave Helen a memorable sendoff.

AVA AND LEON

"That's it, fellas. Helen gave it to me before she died."

"That is a hell of a lot of money. Would you be interested in being a manager if we find something interesting?"

"I don't know. It would depend."

"We could buy up the rest of the block and decide later."

"That's not a bad idea. We could move Mama's Place over here and rent out that building. In fact, that shoe repair next door can be had for a song. We could expand the downstairs and put a new tenant in there."

"I think what you need is professional advice. Find out what complements our neighborhood."

Three national outfits were contacted. The cheapest firm asked for $20,000. So Roy conducted his own survey. After two weeks he concluded more apartments would fit the bill. They were already managing eighteen units so they had the experience with renovations and leasing. Another business was often mentioned, so Roy went to seek advice from Jake.

"A lot of people asked about a grocery store. We could buy an old building and renovate the place. I would rather rent than spend time stocking shelves. What do you think?"

"A mom-and-pop place would be cool. See if you can scare up a couple like that."

Roy spent two weeks asking questions and interviewing prospects. Finally, he found a middle-aged Jewish couple that were a pair of jewels.

"So, Hymie, you think you can stay awake at the cash register?"

"Only if you shut your bagel trap and stop driving me **messhuggenek, aready**."

"But, Hymie, you fall asleep even when I'm quiet as a temple mouse."

"That's because I'm exhausted from searching for peace and quiet, Ava."

"But, Hymie, you sleep every afternoon. You miss your favorite soap operas."

"My life is a soap opera."

"I love you, Hymie. We are a soap opera, just like that Jewish couple on the telly."

"Nine to six is the best time to be open. That's when most people shop their meats and vegetables."

"Yes, Mister Jones. My Hymie is very responsible with money."

A building was purchased within walking distance of The Gridiron. Walls were torn out and the place soon resembled a grocery store. The Goldsteins turned out to be perfect. Women often lingered talking with Ava about Jewish recipes. The men enjoyed Hymie's tales about Israel and the old days.

Another apartment building was purchased and the 40 units renovated with new bathrooms and new kitchens. Comparable rents were $3,000 a month so Roy and Jake held theirs down to $2,000. The building filled up with young couples and business people in seven days. Mika became the manager. By now the police had taken notice of the change in East Harlem so they watched over the area like mother hens. Kids could play in the streets now without armed escorts, and couples strolled the sidewalks at night with no fear of muggers or getting shot.

It was a happy time in all their lives for 17 years. People came and went. Others passed away. The malady affecting Roy came on slowly until he knew it was time to move on. Alzheimer's is a relentless disease that steals one's identity and eventually one's life. He called a meeting with Mika, Luther and Ann, Nadine and Big Jake.

"What I have will take me down in a few more years so I want to leave now while I'm still able to drive. I've picked out a place in Townsend, Tennessee. It's a boarding house where I plan to spend the rest of my days. It's very pretty there. You're welcome to come visit. I have a good deal of money in the bank which I want you to share. I'll keep enough for me. The rest is for you and our neighborhood."

Mika had tears in her eyes. So did the others.

Jake spoke. "We've come a long ways together. Without you, the neighborhood would never have changed. The whole place is in your debt, Roy. Never forget that. If you ever need anything, anything at all, you call me. Write my number on the wall if your memory starts to fade. I'll be right here."

With tears streaming down her cheeks, Mika held Roy's hand. "I love you, Roy. You're the brother I never had. We all love you. The Sky Chief will have a special place for you in the great hereafter."

Detective Ellison: "I'm gonna ride down with you to make sure you get there in one piece. I'd like to see Townsend. I'll catch a plane ride back."

Roy gave his money and his belongings away. Two days later he and Ellison were on the road. Mika and Jake cried when they drove away heading south out of New York.

One door was closing. Another door was about to open.

Part III
The Boarding House

An old man was sitting in front of his computer in a small dimly lit room in Townsend, Tennessee. He was trying to recall events in his life to write them down so he could remember. He was 86 and going blind from glaucoma, and his memory was fading with Alzheimer's. He was a former Marine. He knew that much but the rest of it remained a mystery shrouded in the fog of time. It made him sad that he couldn't remember the names of his friends.

He remembered the Civil War. There had been four of them that always stayed together. He recalled a bolt action rifle with a telescopic sight, but the names of his friends refused to reveal themselves. He took a sip of bourbon whiskey and stared out the window.

A few miles beyond his window panes were the Smoky Mountains. Townsend was a beautiful place in the fall when the leaves were turning colors. He enjoyed early mornings when the fog was rising off the mountains and the deer came for the corn he put out for them. He had nuts for the squirrels and stale bread for the birds. His favorite bird was a crow who called to him from a perch in the treetops. He always gave the crow a little extra.

This evening, like so many other evenings, he sat wondering why so much had changed and why he was still alive. He thought about his mother and father and how they had given him so much when he was a young man. He was spoiled and selfish until he joined the Marine Corps. He learned to appreciate his parents there but they were already gone. He missed them terribly.

Tap, tap, tap. It was the elderly black lady who owned the boarding house.

"Time to eat, Mister Roy. Soup's on."

"Yes, ma'am. I'm coming."

The dining room was old and comfortable with handmade curtains and long-ago pictures on the walls of when Elizabeth was a young woman. The dining room table was cherry wood with a faded World's Fair tablecloth. There were six wooden chairs. One of the chairs was empty because the old man who sat there had passed away the week before. Miss Elizabeth, the owner, sat at the north end of the table and Mister Roy sat at the south end. A retired school teacher sat on the east side where the empty chair was located. A retired fireman and an 80-year-old forest ranger sat in the west chairs.

Miss Elizabeth said the blessing.

"Lord Jesus, we miss Mister Tommy and pray you find him a nice place to live in the Kingdom. He was a sailorman back in the day so a home by an ocean would be good. Thank you for dying on the cross for our souls. Deliver us from sin and show us the Christian way. Bless this food we are about to receive. Ah-man."

"Miss Mary, did you find that library book you wanted?"

"Why, yes, I did. Thank you for asking."

"What's it about?"

"It's about a man called Bass Reeves. He was the first black U.S. Marshal west of the Mississippi River. Mister Reeves was a former slave. It's believed the Lone Ranger was patterned after him."

"I sure never heard that one before."

"My literary club meets once a month at the Maryville Library. They brought it up."

The veteran looked down at his plate, wondering if anything was left in the kitchen. He knows there won't be so he cuts his cornbread in half and wraps it in a napkin. Out on the front porch, he sits on the steps waiting for the skunk. She always comes just before dark. He sees her emerge from the forest. She waddles across the yard and waits at his feet. He places the cornbread in front of his little friend.

With daylight fading he sees them standing at the corner of the yard in front of the trees. Three ghostly figures dressed in fatigues, always looking back at him. They never wave or beckon, they just stand there. He wonders if he's hallucinating. He knows they're his dead comrades, but they never communicate. When they first appeared he tried talking to them, but when he walked toward them they disappeared. He shrugs his shoulders, bids them goodnight, and returns to his room.

Back at his desk, he picks up a framed photograph of four men standing in front of a barracks building. A big man is standing on the right and he's beside the big fellow. The other two men are about his same size. Then he remembered.

The big man was his best friend, Master Sergeant James Buckner. The other two are Lakota Kidwell and John Browning. They were standing on the edge of the clearing a few minutes ago. They're dead now, but they keep coming to visit. He looks out his window again but they're gone now. He wonders if maybe he's going crazy, but he doesn't feel like he's losing his mind. His back hurts but that's arthritis.

What the hell is going on? It doesn't make sense. Why are they here? Do they want something from me? Do I need something from them? I wish I could talk to them. He stretches out on the twin bed to rest his back. Soon he drifts away and dreams.

.... He pushed the sharp end of the tire tool inside the neck of the padlock then twists the lock and metal keeper off the wooden door. He threw those into the bushes behind the building. Five teenagers enter the structure. It was a small grocery located in Vestal in the poor section of South Knoxville.

The cash register was open so they took the silver from the till, throwing the pennies on the floor. There was ham and cheese in the floor cooler so they took some with them to eat. Ronnie loaded up with cartons of cigarettes he would sell at the high school. Then they took off downtown with Jeep, who was AWOL from the Paratroops. They broke open a pay phone on their way to the bus terminal and gave the money to Jeep. He was going back to turn himself in so he needed cash for bus fare. The teens returned to their parked automobiles and drove home.

Rebel Without a Cause was a picture show with James Dean in the 1950s about teenagers rebelling against the norms of society. Roy and his band of delinquents were no different. There was no rhyme or reason to the mischief they spawned upon society. Nor did they give a second thought to the old couple whose store they robbed or the pay phone or anything else besides their own dysfunctional personalities.

The old man opened his eyes. He had been asleep two hours. The dream disturbed him. They always did when he recalled his troubled youth. It made him ashamed and sad and sometimes brought tears to his eyes, remembering the hurt he visited upon his mother and father. He often thought that if he could change part of his life he would change all of it, except the Marine Corps.

He went to his desk and wrote down the names he had remembered. There was a second framed picture beside his monitor with two men and a pretty black girl. One of the men was black, a big fellow, but he couldn't remember their names either.

The next morning he had just finished shaving when Miss Elizabeth rang the cowbell for breakfast. When he sat down at the table he was delighted to see what Elizabeth had prepared, biscuits and gravy with bacon and fried potatoes and coffee. She had sold some of the honey she put up in Mason jars from her bee hives in the backyard. The five of them began talking all at once over their approval of a country breakfast.

After a second cup of coffee, he went outside to feed the animals. The deer were waiting in the front yard and so were the squirrels, four of them. He poured corn in three separate bowls then sat down on his wooden stool to feed the squirrels. The crow was perched nearby and talking up a storm. He tossed a slice of bread out in the yard and proceeded to attend to the squirrels. They came up to him and he would hand them the nuts. The birds made short work of the bread.

Miss Elizabeth always watched from the front porch. Sometimes the others did too but they were used to it by now so they usually went about their business. Miss Elizabeth loved the animals the same as the old man.

Back in his room, he picked up the piece of paper with the names on it, remembering a time when he and Gunny killed nine men in cold blood. They were Progressives who had raped a young wife then murdered the couple and took what little food they had. The men were sitting around a campfire eating when he and Gunny came out of the woods behind them. They made excuses about what they had done, saying over and over they were just following orders. He and Gunny switched their weapons to full automatic and cut them down like rabid animals.

There were other times too but one in particular stood out. It was the winter of '26 when the four of them had cornered an enemy force of about 20 men in a box canyon in Alabama. It was an enemy fueling station filled with volatile drums of fuel oil and gasoline. The enemy soldiers asked them not to shoot, saying they would surrender. The four Marines opened fire causing one of the drums to explode. The whole place went up in boiling mushrooms of fire.

They had vowed never to take prisoners following the incident at the orphanage where the children had been brutalized and murdered, but the twisted faces of dying men never left his dreams. He wondered if growing old made him a pussy. He discussed this with Miss Margaret. She told him about being a little black girl growing up in a small southern town where black people were referred to as niggers and jungle bunnies. She hated those racist white people. But when she got older she understood that most everyone is just the same, except for a few bad ones. She said governments are like that, lying and starting wars, training their citizens to kill other citizens. Roy thought about that one a spell and decided she was a doggone smart lady.

That evening after supper he went back outside to feed his little skunk friend. Miss Margaret sat on the porch and watched. He had fresh lettuce. He laid the crisp green lettuce before the skunk then went back to sit on the porch with Miss Margaret.

"Mister Roy, you were a cook in the Marines, weren't you?"

"Yes, ma'am, I was."

"Could you help out in the kitchen?"

PART III

"Why sure, is something wrong?"

"I wants to tell you something but I want you to promise you won't tell none of the others."

"You have my word."

"I'm sick. I got the cancer. My doctor tells me I ain't got much longer."

"I got a little money. Would a specialist help?"

"No, honey, ain't nobody can help. I got the stuff all over me."

"Are you in pain? Do you have pain pills?"

"I takes one in the mornin' an' one in the evenin'. It keeps the wolf away from my door."

"How long did the doctor say?"

"Three or four months, maybe less."

"I'll do anything I can to help. Do you need anything?"

"I wants to be buried in the Negro cemetery in Louisville. It's right behind that gas station on Topside Road. My mama is buried there. I got a plot paid for beside Mama. The papers are on top of my dresser. I wants you to see to it."

"Do you have a preacher?"

"I ain't got no preacher."

"I'll get my Marine Corps pastor."

"Lord, honey, you done took a load off my mind. I'm leavin' this house to you 'cause I ain't got no kin left. Take care of the others long as you can. They're like my own flesh and blood."

That weekend Roy went into Maryville and withdrew $1,000 from Smart Bank. The following Monday Miss Margaret and her boarders were treated to orange juice, filet mignon, fried eggs, hash brown potatoes with Vidalia onions, and buttered biscuits with cherry preserves. Dessert was apple pie á la mode.

Five weeks later Miss Margaret went into the hospital.

MISS MARGARET

Margaret was on the fourth floor of Blount Memorial Hospital in Maryville. The sheriff's office is across the street. It was Sunday and visiting hours were open.

"I brought you a couple uh magazines."

"Give 'em to the old lady next door. I don't read that nonsense. I would like to have my Bible. And could you bring me a piece of your pie? If the cancer don't kill me, the food in here will."

"I'll cook you a meal and bring it up. Anything special you want?"

"Oh my goodness gracious …. Let me see now, tomato pudding, fried okra, mashed potatoes and gravy, lots uh gravy. And some pie. Oh, an' a pan of your cornbread."

"I'll come back tomorrow. I'll have 'em hot it up downstairs in the kitchen."

"Bless you, Mister Roy. You sho' is a good 'un."

"Do you have any pain?"

"No, honey, my morphine drip takes care of that. Makes me itch some. The nurse said that's normal."

"The pastor said he'd come and visit any time you like."

"Ask him to come visit me next week."

"The crew all sends you their best wishes. I told 'em about the cancer. They're bent out of shape your bein' in here an' all. We all miss you."

"I'm going to a better place pretty soon. I don't know if you can miss folks in Heaven, but if you do I'll miss them too. And you, Mister Roy. You're the nicest man I've ever known. Don't fret none about the past, mistakes you made, men you killed. God has a special place for men like you and your three friends. I'll put in a good word when I get up there."

"There should be more women like you, Miss Margaret. Your intelligence and humor reminds me of my mother and father. I wish it had rubbed off on me sooner, but some of it did, finally. I'll be along one of these days to visit you and my mom and dad. Maybe I can make tomato pudding in Heaven."

The next afternoon he arrived with a covered tray, which he sat down on a wheelchair. He rolled the chair down to the kitchen where they warmed it up. Wheeling it into an elevator, he pushed the button for the fourth floor. When he entered her room he found her bed empty.

Roy set the tray on the bed, sat down in the wheelchair, lay his face and arms down on the white sheet and wept. He cried until the nurses came to see what was wrong.

BOOK CLUB

Another month went by. Roy was busy in the kitchen three times a day. One morning Miss Mary came in and asked him a question.

"Would you and the men like to join my literary group? There aren't but a few of us but we have interesting discussions about authors and their novels. Nothing much goes on here in Townsend so I thought you might be interested."

"Well, I don't know. Why don't you bring it up tonight over supper?"

Miss Mary did and to her surprise the fireman and the forest ranger were enthusiastic. She was the youngest of the four so she drove them to the library for the monthly meeting. The president of the club chose a book he thought would interest the newcomers.

"John Steinbeck published *The Moon Is Down* in 1942. It's a fictional account of a coastal town in Northern Europe occupied by a fictional army. In reality, it was a subtle blueprint about resistance against the Nazis. Your assignment for next month is to read the novel and share your thoughts about its meaning."

The fireman, the forest ranger, and Roy were all three enthused over the assignment. Miss Mary was delighted that her charges had taken an interest in her literary club. Discussing books at the dinner table became a social event. They talked often about Miss Margaret and how she had brought them together as a family. Growing old wasn't so lonely when there was someone there who understood.

GOING HOME

.... the dream was vivid and real. Carlos had taken a bullet and was dying. Roy held him in his arms while the warm blood ran down over his hands. Carlos was trying to talk but the shadows, he called them, were closing in. Finally, his heart stopped beating and Carlos was gone. Roy woke up crying.

"I don't see much sense in my hanging around here anymore. I'm old and used up. Mary can cook for the guys. I better go to the courthouse and put this place in her name. I want to visit Miss Margaret, see my parents again."

So he took a taxi to the courthouse and wrote a quitclaim deed in Mary Snyder's name. Then he went by Smart Bank and closed his account and returned to the boarding house. When supper was over he went outside with the little skunk.

"I left a note for Mary. She'll be looking after you from now on. Goodbye, my little friend."

He reached inside his shirt pocket and took out a paper packet with a capsule inside. He had been given the pill in Tel Aviv in case he was captured. Suicide was a far better fate than being tortured for days by Arab fanatics. He swallowed the tablet with a chaser of bourbon and Coca-Cola.

It only took a minute for the drowsiness to set in. There was no pain. He was falling down a long dark tunnel into a black void. When he opened his eyes he was with his friends over on the side of the front yard. He looked back and saw his body slumped over on the porch floor. The little skunk was there sitting at his feet.

"We waited for ya. We're going with you."

"Thanks, fellas. I'm going to visit my mother and father."

About the Author
Larry Henry

Larry Henry was born in 1938. Unemployment was 19%. The Depression was once again gaining momentum. Hitler had marched into Austria while Imperial Japan was running amok in China. Then in 1941 Japan bombed Pearl Harbor and President Roosevelt declared war on Japan. Four days later Hitler declared war on the United States. WWII brought America out of the Great Depression.

The 1940s were glory years. But the best years America ever saw were the 1950s. They had Elvis and James Dean, Little Richard, Patsy Cline, Nat King Cole, and Humphrey Bogart. John Wayne was there, black and white TV, drive-in restaurants, nuclear power, and John Ford. There was Brando and Maureen O'Hara, Ole Blue Eyes, and Marilyn Monroe. God was in every public school and so was the pledge of allegiance. Jobs grew on trees. A crack had opened in the universe, and the cosmic images and events that came through can never be duplicated ever again. Henry and his friends didn't know it then but those images and events changed them forever. They were the children of the Greatest Generation, and in their own "rebel without a cause" way they too assumed greatness. No generation since has ever come close to those magical bygone days of yesteryear.

ABOUT THE AUTHOR

Larry Henry joined the Marine Reserves in 1957. Parris Island was a rude awakening for this young boy from South Knoxville, TN, but it opened his eyes to the mighty American Armed Forces and events to come in Vietnam and beyond. When a Democrat-controlled Congress refused to release the B52's in 1975, South Vietnam went down to defeat. Henry suspected something was not right so he began to read and study. All roads led back to Washington, DC.

At first, he blamed the Democrats but there was plenty enough RINOs to go around. Korea had been a draw, Vietnam was a bloody mistake. This was not the American way. He didn't understand until he began following the money. Turns out a lot of corrupt politicians and businessmen and women were getting rich off those half-assed wars.

.... So Larry Henry wrote his last three books as a warning about what could happen.

The 2020 election was stolen by the Democrats. Barack Obama had a hand in this, Nancy Pelosi, the DNC, and a host of others including Fake News and the FBI. What followed was an introduction to centralized government and Big Brother. Turning the other cheek is a fine Christian belief, but it does not work with communism. Washington, DC is awash with Useful Idiots. Capitol Hill is owned and operated by a treasonous anti-American bureaucracy, They must never again be allowed inside our White House.

Donald Trump is the Winston Churchill of the 21st Century. Churchill saved the world from the evil Nazis in Germany. Donald Trump is saving the world from the wicked communists in America.

Lightning Source LLC
LaVergne TN
LVHW020412070526
838199LV00054B/3585